# THE USBORNE COMPLETE BOOK OF
# THE INTERNET &
# WORLD WIDE WEB

## *Philippa Wingate and Asha Kalbag*

*Design and DTP by Russell Punter, Isaac Quaye,
Andy Griffin, Michael Wheatley and Zöe Wray
Illustrations by Andy Griffin
Additional Illustrations by Isaac Quaye*

*Technical consultants: Liam Devany, Nick Bell
Additional consultancy by Lisa Hughes, Thomas Barry,
Michael Sullivan and Artemis Interactive
Photography by Howard Allman
Edited by Philippa Wingate and Jane Chisholm
Managing designers: Stephen Wright and Mary Cartwright*

# About this book

The Internet, also known as the Net, can seem huge and confusing. Every day you'll hear people talking about it, using jargon, buzzwords and technobabble.

Don't panic. As new software is developed and better techniques for exploring the Internet are introduced, it's becoming an easier place to find your way around. This book will make it even easier.

## Net knowledge

*The Usborne Complete Book of the Internet & World Wide Web* introduces you to the Net. It tells you what it is, how it works and describes the fun and interesting things you can find on it.

There is a section telling you how to go "on-line" yourself, which means getting connected to the Net. It details what equipment and software you need, and how to find a company which will give you access to the Net.

This book introduces the main facilities the Net offers, and shows you how to use the programs that help you to explore them. There is an extensive section on the World Wide Web, probably the most exciting part of the Net.

## Getting on the Net yourself

This book doesn't just help you understand the Net, it shows you how to become part of it.

Pages 52 to 81 will show you how to create your own documents to go on the Net. Clear instructions and illustrated examples guide you through how to construct personal "pages". There's information about the programs and computer code you will need to use, and advice about how to transfer your finished pages onto the Net.

## Hot spots

On pages 96 and 97 there's a selection of some of the useful things you will find on the Net.

The Internet and its technology are changing rapidly. Information about it goes out of date quickly. Some things on the Net change or disappear, so it's difficult to guarantee that all the references in this book will remain correct. There is, however, lots of basic information that will be invaluable to a new user.

## Net software

There are many different Internet software packages available. At the time of writing, Netscape Navigator® and Microsoft® Internet Explorer were the most popular programs for exploring the Net, and they are used for the sample screens shown in this book.

If you have a computer already set up to use the Internet, you may have a different program installed, or a different version of the programs used in this book. Don't worry. Internet programs are often very similar. Using the examples in this book as a guide, you will be able to figure out how to use your own programs, even if some of their buttons and menu items have slightly different names.

Alternatively, on page 44, you can find out how to get your own copy of the Netscape Navigator or Microsoft Internet Explorer programs from the Net.

# What is the Internet?

The Internet is a vast computer network linking together millions of smaller networks all over the world.

On these pages you can find out exactly what a network is and how the computers on the Internet are connected to one another.

## What is a network?

A network is the name given to a group of computers and computer equipment that have been joined together so they can share information and resources. The computers in an office, for example, are often networked so that they can use the same files and printers.

All the computers linked to the Internet can exchange information with each other. It's as easy to communicate with a computer on the other side of the world as with one that is right next door.

Once your own computer is connected to the Net it is like a spider in the middle of a huge web. All the threads of the web can bring you information from other computers.

## Servers and clients

There are two main types of computers on the Internet. The ones which store, sort and distribute information are called hosts, or servers. Those that access and use this information, such as your computer at home, are called clients. A server computer serves a client computer, like a store owner helping a customer.

*The picture below shows how the computer networks in different organizations in a town are linked together by the Net.*

*People can connect their computers at home to the Net.*

*At school, children can use the Net to learn and communicate with children in other countries.*

*Universities all over the world can use the Net to share their research information.*

*Cables link one computer network to another.*

*People can use the computers at this special café to access the Net.*

## Telephone lines

The computer networks that make up the Net are linked together by private and public telephone systems. They can send and receive information along telephone lines. These lines range from cables made of twisted copper wires, to cables containing glass strands, that can carry lots of data at high speeds (over a thousand times faster than copper phone lines). Some networks can be linked by radio waves and microwaves. Networks in different countries and continents are often joined by undersea cables or by satellites.

*This computer belongs to a company that provides people at home or in offices with Net access.*

*Businesses can use the Net to sell their products.*

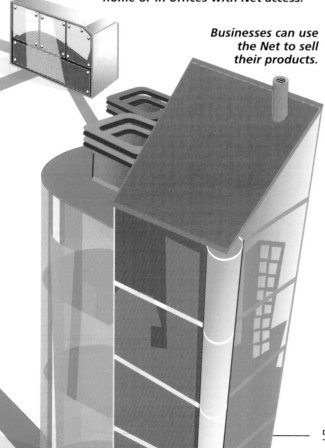

*Cables can run under seas and oceans.*

*The largest computers on the Net are connected by links known as backbones.*

## Connections

Some computers, especially ones used in large organizations such as universities, government departments and big businesses, have a "dedicated" Net connection. This means that they are linked to the Net all the time.

People using computers in homes and offices usually don't have dedicated connections. They can join or "hook up" to the Net by using the telephone to dial up a connection with a computer that is already on-line.

### 🌐 How big?

From huge supercomputers to small personal computers, all kinds of computers make up the Net. There are already tens of millions of host computers, and every month three million new hosts and almost 50,000 networks are added to it. These figures are increasing rapidly.

# What's on the Net?

From games to gossip, messages to music, and shopping to academic research, once you have access to the Internet, you can do a huge variety of things. These pages show you just some of them.

## Information

There are many computers on the Net storing millions of files of information which are free for you to use. There are cartoons, art galleries, magazines and information which could help you with your work or hobbies.

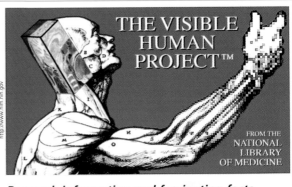

Research information and fascinating facts.

Send messages.

Read a selection of cartoons.

Communicate by Internet telephone.

Listen to music or news on Internet radio.

Join in guided tours around museums and monuments.

Look at beautiful pictures and photographs.

## Communication

There are millions of Net users all over the world with whom you can communicate, for work or for pleasure. You can send messages, chat, or take part in debates and discussions with other people who share your interests.

## Services

Some computers on the Net provide you with services. You can use them to order flowers, get financial advice, find out train or airline times, book tickets for a show, check the weather report and catch some up-to-date news.

Play a wide selection of games.

Use a video telephone.

Enjoy lots of great music and fan clubs.

Get a variety of financial information.

Find things just for kids.

Check train timetables and ticket prices.

Look at up-to-date weather forecasts.

## Programs

There are lots of programs available for you to copy onto your computer. Some are free to use; others you'll need to pay for. There are programs for playing games, listening to music or watching videos, as well as the latest programs to help you use the Net more efficiently.

## Surfing

Cyberspace is the name given to the imaginary space you travel in when you use the Net. Even though you stay in one place, you make an imaginary journey around the world by linking up to computers in different places. Moving around the Net is also known as "surfing".

# How does the Net work?

Before two computers on the Internet can exchange information, they need to be able to find each other and communicate in a language that they can both understand.

## Name and number

To enable computers on the Net to locate each other, they have unique addresses, called Internet Protocol (IP) addresses. IP addresses take the form of numbers. Numbers are difficult to remember, so each computer is also given a name, known as its domain name. The name has three main sections that give information about where the computer is located. Each section is separated by a dot.

Here's an imaginary domain name:

**usborne.co.uk** *This name tells you what organization the user works in.*

**usborne.co.uk** *This identifies the type of organization.*

**usborne.co.uk** *This tells you the geographical location or country.*

## Country codes

Many countries have their own code. Here are some you may come across:

**au** Australia
**ca** Canada
**de** Germany
**fr** France
**nl** Netherlands
**se** Sweden
**uk** United Kingdom

If an address has no country code, this usually indicates that a computer is in the USA.

## Organizations

Here's a list of some of the codes for the types of organizations found in domain names:

**ac** an academic organization
**co** or **com** a commercial organization
**edu** an educational institution
**gov** a government body
**net** an organization involved in running the Net
**org** a non profit-making organization

## Computer talk

To make sure that all the computers on the Net can communicate with each other, they all use the same language. It is called TCP/IP (Transmission Control Protocol/Internet Protocol).

TCP/IP ensures that when data is sent from one computer to another, it is transmitted in a particular way and that it arrives safely in the right place. If, for example, one computer sends a picture to another computer, the picture is broken down into small "packets" of data. Each packet includes information about where it has come from and where it is going to. The packets travel via the Net to the destination computer where they are reassembled.

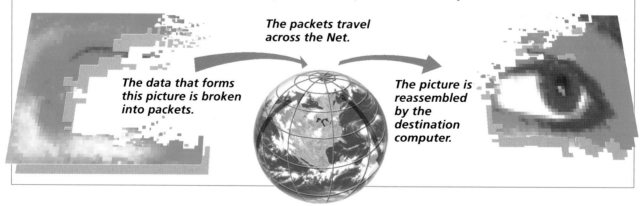

*The packets travel across the Net.*

*The data that forms this picture is broken into packets.*

*The picture is reassembled by the destination computer.*

# Net history

Here's a brief history of how the Net began and how it became the worldwide network that it is today.

**1960s** The US Defense Department launched a project to design a computer network that could withstand nuclear attack. If part of the network was destroyed, information could be transmitted to its destination by alternative routes. The network became known as ARPANET (Advanced Research Projects Agency NETwork).

**1970s** Supercomputers in universities and companies throughout America were linked so that they could share research information.

**1980s** A new network called NSFNET (National Science Foundation NETwork) was set up.

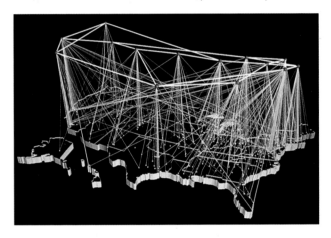

*This diagram shows the main connections on the NSFNET on a map of the USA.*

NSFNET was a network exchanging non-commercial information.

**1990s** The network was opened up to everyone, including commercial companies and people using computers at home. The World Wide Web (see page 27) made the Net easier to use and, as a result, it expanded rapidly.

## Who controls the Net?

Despite constant attempts by many governments and large organizations, nobody actually controls the Net. It is made up of lots of individual networks which are owned by somebody, but nobody owns all of it.

## A test run on the Net

Now that you know the basics of what the Internet is and how it works, you should try it out.

You may find you belong to an organization that is already on-line. Many schools, colleges and universities have networks linked to the Net. Alternatively, you may work in an office that has computers on-line.

If you can't gain access in this way, ask a friend who is on-line to give you a demonstration.

You might find a local museum or library has Net access. Some bookstores and computer stores have computers on which you can explore the Net.

Another good way of trying out the Net is to go to a cybercafé. These are special cafés where you can pay to use computers that are connected to the Net.

*This cybercafé is located in the Centre Georges Pompidou, in Paris.*

# Getting connected: the hardware

On these pages you can find out exactly what equipment you need to use the Net.

## A computer

**A multimedia PC**

**Speakers allow you to hear sounds on Web pages.**

**A mouse**

**Web pages appear on your computer screen or "monitor".**

You don't need a brand new computer to use the Internet. If you have a PC which has at least a 386 processor chip, you will be able to connect to the Internet. If you are using a Macintosh, your computer needs a 8036 chip or better.

Your computer needs a lot of RAM (Random Access Memory). RAM is the part of your computer's memory which enables it to use programs. Memory is measured in bytes, and 1 megabyte (MB) is just over a million bytes. Your computer needs at least 16MB of RAM to use Internet software (you can find out about this software on pages 12 and 13).

Software, and any other information you want to save permanently, is stored on your computer's hard disk. Your computer needs at least 200MB of free hard disk space to store Net and Web software. (Free space is storage space that isn't being used by other programs.)

## A modem

The easiest way to join up your computer to the Net is by using a telephone line.

There are two main ways of sending information across telephone networks. It can be sent either in the form of sound waves, which are called analog signals, or as electronic pulses, which are called digital signals.

A computer produces data in digital form. To communicate over analog telephone lines, it needs a device called a modem. A modem converts digital signals into analog signals and back again.

Ask the company that provides you with a telephone service what kind of telephone lines your telephone uses. If it uses analog lines, you will need a modem.

*This picture shows two computers on the Internet exchanging information using modems.*

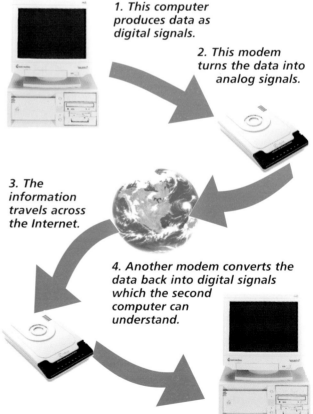

**1. This computer produces data as digital signals.**

**2. This modem turns the data into analog signals.**

**3. The information travels across the Internet.**

**4. Another modem converts the data back into digital signals which the second computer can understand.**

## Which modem?

There are two types of modems that can be used with desktop computers: internal modems and external modems.

An internal modem fits inside your computer's processing unit. An external modem sits on your desktop. It has a cable which plugs into one of the sockets in your computer's processing unit. This socket is called a serial port.

## Modem speed

Modems transfer data to and from the Net at different speeds. The speed is measured in bits per second (bps). It is best to buy the fastest modem you can afford. Make sure it works at no less than 28,800 bps. If you have a high-speed modem you will spend less time waiting for Web pages to appear on your screen.

## A telephone line

You must be able to plug your modem into a telephone point. To do this, you may have to move your computer or use an extension lead.

If you have only one telephone line, you won't be able to receive or make telephone calls while you are connected to the Internet.

## Special Internet computers

If you don't already own a computer, and only want one to access the Internet, you may consider buying a Network Computer (NC). These machines are less expensive than ordinary computers because they only allow you to use the Internet. They are not as powerful as ordinary computers and rely on other computers on the Internet to store and process data for them.

## Extra hardware

If you want to use the Net for a specific purpose, such as watching video clips or playing games, you may need to add some extra hardware to your computer.

**Video** To enjoy the animation and videos that are available on the Net, your computer needs a powerful graphics card. If your computer doesn't have the right kind of card, the pictures will be fuzzy and will move slowly.

All Macintoshes and most PCs with Pentium processors contain suitable graphics cards. Otherwise you may need to buy a better card. To watch videos, you need at least a 32 bit card with 2MB of Video RAM (VRAM).

**Sound** If you want to hear sounds on the Net, your computer must have a sound card. This is a device which enables your computer to produce sound. Macintoshes and multimedia PCs already contain sound cards and speakers. If you have another kind of computer you may need to have these added.

*Sound cards*

**Gaming equipment** If you want to play some of the games available on the Net, you will find it easier with a joystick. For games in which you pretend to control a vehicle, a driving wheel. may be useful.

*A driving wheel*

---
11

# Getting connected: the software

To use the Internet, you will need to add some special programs to your computer. In this section you will find out what these programs are and how you can obtain them.

## A browser

The most important program you will need is called a browser. This is a program which allows you to look at information on the World Wide Web (see page 27). Most browsers also allow you to send messages to other users, copy files from the Net and join in discussion groups.

A browser window has two main parts: a central area where information is displayed, and a panel with various buttons and menus. (Find out how to open your browser window on page 27.)

Two popular browsers are Netscape Navigator and Microsoft® Internet Explorer. Their windows are shown below.

## Which browser?

This book explains how to use both Netscape Navigator and Microsoft Internet Explorer to explore the Net. Wherever necessary, there are two sets of instructions for the same activity.

If you have Netscape Navigator, follow the instructions next to this icon.

If you are using Microsoft Internet Explorer, follow the instructions next to this icon.

Don't worry if you have another browser, or a different version of the browsers used here. Most browsers have the same basic functions, so you should be able to work out how to use the one you have quite easily.

**The Netscape Navigator window**

*Menu bar*

*The tool bar buttons help you to find your way around the Web.*

*Menu bar*

**Documents on the Web are displayed in this area.**

**The Microsoft Internet Explorer window**

## Browser updates

Companies that make browsers are continually improving their programs. The first browsers available to Net users could only show words and still pictures, but newer versions can handle more complicated methods of showing information, such as moving pictures.

To enjoy new and exciting ways in which information is presented on Web pages, you will need to keep updating your browser. You can use the Web to copy a more recent version of your browser off the Internet onto your computer. (Find out how to copy software off the Net on pages 44 to 47.)

## Looking good

Some Web pages have been "optimized" for a particular browser. This means they look and work better when you look at them with that browser.

You can still look at an optimized page with another browser, but you will not be able to see all the decorative features. If there is enough space on your computer's hard disk, you may want to keep more than one browser on your computer, so that you can always see pages at their best.

## Additional software

There are other programs that you will need in order to use the Internet.

Your computer needs a "dialer". This is a program which enables it to operate your modem and connect to the Net.

You may also need a program which allows your computer to communicate with other Internet computers.

You will need programs for sending electronic mail (see page 17) and for joining in discussion groups called newsgroups (see page 22), and for copying files off the Net onto your own computer. Many browsers enable you to do all these things, but you can buy separate programs too.

## Obtaining the software you need

Internet software is sometimes given away with Internet magazines. Most people, however, obtain it from an "access provider". This is a company that you pay in order to gain access to the Internet (see pages 14 and 15).

An access provider has computers which are permanently linked to the Net. It allows you to connect your computer to one of these. If you make this connection using a telephone line, it is called a dial-up connection.

When you open an account with an access provider, they will send you a CD or floppy disks containing a browser and all the other software you need to use the Net. Make sure you tell them what kind of computer you have so they send you the correct software. (You can find out how to choose an access provider on pages 14 and 15.)

## Installing your software

To install your Internet software, carefully follow the instructions included with it.

A message will appear on your screen telling you if the installation has been successful. If you have any problems, call your access provider's helpline for advice. The telephone number of the helpline should be sent to you with the software.

# Providing access

Unless the computer you are using is permanently connected to the Net, you will need to pay a company to give you access. This company will act as your gateway to the Net by allowing you to hook up to their computers which are connected to the Net.

Two main types of companies offer this service: Internet access providers and on-line services.

## Internet access providers

A company that provides access to the Net is called an Internet access provider (IAP) or an Internet service provider (ISP). There are many different companies available and more are appearing all the time. You will need to open an account with one. Some may offer you a free trial period of connection to the Net.

## On-line services

An on-line service is a company that provides you with access to its own private network in addition to access to the Internet itself. The types of services offered on private networks range from international news to shopping facilities, business information, discussion groups, and a wide selection of entertainments.

## Making choices

You'll find the phone numbers of a selection of Internet service providers and on-line services advertised in Internet magazines and local newspapers, with details of any special offers available. Each company offers different services, software and costs.

Phone up a company to make sure that they will provide the service best suited to your needs. Here are some of the key questions to ask:

**Can I access your computer for the cost of a local call?**
Large access providers have points of access to the Net all over the country. Each of these is called a node, or a

Point of Presence (POP).

Make sure that the access provider you choose has a POP near you, so that you only have to pay for a local telephone call to go on-line. This will be far cheaper than making a long distance call every time you use the Net.

**What will my e-mail* address be?**
Each Net user is given a unique address for sending and receiving e-mail. Some people like to use their name or nickname as part of their e-mail address.

Ask an access provider how much choice they can give you in choosing an address.

**What costs can I expect?**
Make sure that you understand exactly how much you will have to pay for your Internet connection. There is a list of the type of charges you can expect on page 15.

Try to avoid paying start-up costs, as you will lose this money if you decide to change access providers.

Find out whether there is a monthly fee and whether you will be charged for the amount of time you spend on-line.

If you are using an on-line service, check what fee you will have to pay for using their special services and their private network.

*You can find out about e-mail on page 17.*

## Costs

Different companies have different structures of costs for their services. Here are some of the costs you will come across:

**Start-up cost** – You may have to pay to open an account with an access provider.

**Monthly fees** and **time charges** – In some countries, such as Great Britain, local telephone calls are charged by the second. Most access providers in these countries do not charge for the amount of time a user spends on-line and only charge a small monthly fee for using their services. Many on-line services, however, do charge for time spent on-line.

In countries such as the USA and Australia, where local telephone calls cost a fixed amount or nothing, access providers usually charge for the amount of time a user spends on-line. This discourages people from staying on-line all day, preventing others from using the Net.

**Software** – Some access providers will send you a CD or a number of floppy disks containing all the Internet software you will need to get started. The cost of this is usually included in the start-up fee. Other companies may charge you a fee to copy software from the Net. Find out more about this on page 45.

## Opening an account

Once you have decided to open an account, you'll need to give your access provider your name, address and telephone number.

Make sure that you tell them what kind of computer you are using so that they send you the correct Internet software.

### What software do you supply?
Different companies supply different Internet software. If a friend has recommended a particular program, you may want to ask if it is available.

### Do you provide access for the type and speed of modem I have?
Make sure that the modems (see page 10) used by an access provider can communicate efficiently with your modem.

The speed of the modems they use should not be slower than the speed of the modem connected to your computer.

### Do you have enough modems so that I can connect at peak times?
Each person who dials up an access provider's computer needs a separate modem to make their connection. There are certain times of day when a lot of people use the Net. If all an access provider's modems are being used, you will get a busy signal and won't be able to get a Net connection.

Think about when you are most likely to use the Net and ask the access provider what its busiest periods are. Ask what its modem to customer ratio is.

### Do you have a helpline?
Most access providers have a telephone helpline to give you advice on how to install and use your Internet software. Make sure that this helpline is available at the times when you are most likely to be using the Net, such as during the evening or at weekends.

# Connecting and disconnecting

Once you have your equipment set up and your software installed, you are ready to connect up to the Internet for the first time. If your computer is not permanently connected to the Net, you will need to dial up a connection to your access provider's computer.

## Dialing up a connection

Open your connection software. There may be a button or menu item which tells your modem to dial up a connection. If there isn't, open your Web browser by double-clicking on its icon. Your browser may automatically instruct your modem to connect to the Net. If not, a message will appear asking if your wish to connect. Click *Yes*.

*This is part of the connection window of an access provider called Pipex Dial.*

*The Connect button*

*These buttons will start up your modem and take you straight to a particular Net facility.*

## Password

A box may appear asking you to supply a password. This password will be given to you by your access provider.

## Your modem

Once your modem starts working, you may see flashing lights (if the modem is on your desktop) and hear

Dialing...

dial tones. When it connects to the access provider's computer, you may hear strange squealing and fizzing sounds.

## Connected

Connected

Once you are connected, an icon or message will tell you that your dial-up has been successful.

Call Time
**00:09:08**

Your window may have a display that begins to time how long you have been connected to the Net.

## No connection?

It may be more complicated than you think to get all the software correctly installed and your modem working.

Connection Lost

Don't hesitate to ring up your access provider's helpline with any problems. They should be able to help you.

When you are satisfied that your software and equipment are working, you may still be unable to get a connection. A message may appear saying your dial-up has been unsuccessful. Look at page 86 to find out why this may happen.

## Warning

With some Internet connections you will automatically be given the choice of disconnecting after a certain period of time. This is a safeguard against spending hours on-line and possibly running up an enormous phone bill.

If your software doesn't do this, be careful not to leave your computer connected to the Net for long periods.

## Disconnecting

To disconnect from the Net, select the disconnect button or menu item.

# E-mail

Electronic mail, known as e-mail, is a method of using your computer to send messages to other Net users. It's a great way of communicating. With e-mail you can send messages more quickly and cheaply than normal mail. An e-mail sent from London can arrive in Tokyo in under a minute and only cost the same as a local telephone call. Net users call the normal mail "snail mail" because it's so slow!

## E-mail addresses

With e-mail, as with normal mail, you need to know someone's address before you can send them a message. Everyone on the Net has a unique e-mail address. When you start an account with a access provider you'll be given your own address.

An e-mail address has two main sections: the username and the domain name. The username is usually the name or nickname of the person using e-mail. (One on-line service called CompuServe uses a number instead of a name.)

The username is followed by an **@** symbol, which means "at".

The domain name gives information about the computer and its location. (You can read more about domain names on page 8.)

Here's an imaginary e-mail address:

## philippa@usborne.co.uk

**Username**          **Domain name**          **Country**
          **At**                              **Code**

### @ Take care

Some e-mail addresses are fairly complicated, so make sure that you write them down *very* carefully.

## How does e-mail work?

When you send an e-mail message from your computer, it is delivered to a computer called a mail server. From there, it is transferred across the Net, via a chain of mail servers, until it arrives at its destination.

## E-mail software

The software package supplied by your access provider should include an e-mail program. The one used in the examples in this book is Netscape Mail which is part of Netscape Navigator version 2.01.

If you are using Microsoft Windows 95 or Macintosh System 7, you will probably already have e-mail software installed on your computer.

## An e-mail window

Open your e-mail program window. The example screen shown below is the Netscape Mail window. It shows some of the main parts of an e-mail window. Other e-mail program windows will share many of the same features.

**The Netscape Mail window**

**These are the folders in which incoming and outgoing mail is stored.**

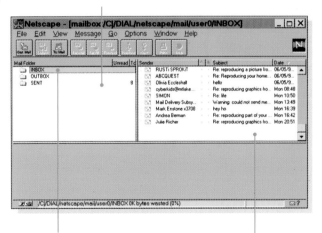

**The INBOX folder is open.**

**This window shows what messages are currently stored in the INBOX folder.**

# Sending e-mail

On these pages you can discover exactly how to send an e-mail to another Net user anywhere in the world. Find out how to create a handy address book for the e-mail addresses of any friends to whom you want to send messages regularly.

## Preparing an e-mail

Open your e-mail program window and select the button or menu item for composing a new message. A window will open. Netscape Mail's Message Composition window is shown below. It consists of a header section and a body section. Type your message into the blank body section. (You will find some advice on writing e-mail on page 26.)

## Filling in a header

Before you can send an e-mail you have to fill in the header section. This is like writing the address on the front of an envelope to make sure the letter inside reaches its destination.

In the *Mail To:* box, type the e-mail address of the person to whom you are sending the message. Add the address of anyone you want to send a copy of your e-mail to in the *CC:* box.

Choose an informative subject line to fill in the *Subject:* box. Many Net users receive lots of e-mail, including junk e-mail which is mostly advertising. Use the subject line to give the person who receives your e-mail an idea of what is contained in your message. This ensures that he or she won't just delete the message without reading it. The subject lines appear in a list of messages stored on your computer. They act as a useful reminder of what each e-mail is about.

**Netscape Mail's Message Composition window**

*The header section*

Click here to send your e-mail.

The e-mail address of the recipient goes here.

The subject line

**Netscape - [Message Composition]**

File  Edit  View  Options  Window

Send  Quote  Attach  Address  Stop

Mail To: philippa@usborne.co.uk

Cc:

Subject: Good luck

Attachment:

Dear Philippa
It was great to see you.
Good luck with the play next week. I hope it goes well. Make sure you break a leg :-)
Let me know when you will be back in the summer and we will meet up again.
Take care.
John

*The body section*

## @Spending money

If you are charged by the minute for the time you are on-line, write your e-mail before you connect up to the Net. You can then take your time to make sure you are happy with your message before you spend money sending it.

## Signing off

Many e-mail programs allow you to create a personal "signature" which automatically appears at the end of your messages.

Your signature can only be made up of letters and symbols from the keyboard. Some people use them to draw complicated pictures, while others will include a funny quotation. You could include the snail mail address and telephone number of your school or company.

The signatures shown below are pretty long. Ideally, you should make your signature no more than four lines. People will have to spend time and money downloading your e-mail file, so a long signature might make you unpopular.

If you want your signature to be included with an e-mail, you have to instruct your computer to attach it.

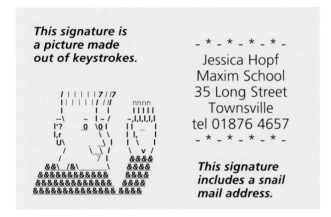

**This signature is a picture made out of keystrokes.**

- * - * - * - * -
Jessica Hopf
Maxim School
35 Long Street
Townsville
tel 01876 4657
- * - * - * - * -

**This signature includes a snail mail address.**

## Sending an e-mail

When you are ready to send an e-mail message, select the send button or menu item.

If you are connected to the Net already, your message should be sent right away. If you aren't connected, your computer will probably save the e-mail. Next time you dial up a Net connection, it will be sent.

*Your e-mail program may show an animation to tell you that your message has been sent.*

## An address book

Many e-mail programs let you create an address book containing the names and e-mail addresses of the people to whom you regularly send messages.

You can type e-mail addresses into your address book, or add addresses from e-mails you have already received.

To send a message to a friend, you usually only have to double-click on their name in your address book. A message composition window that is already addressed to them will open.

**Netscape Mail's Address Book window**

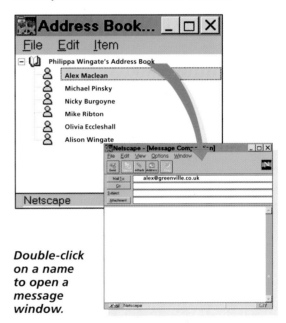

**Double-click on a name to open a message window.**

## Finding an address

There isn't a directory listing the e-mail addresses of all the users on the Net. The easiest way to get someone's address is to call up and ask them. Get them to send you an e-mail to make sure that you don't write down the wrong address. Their address should appear at the top of their message.

# Receiving e-mail

Any e-mail sent to you will be stored in a mailbox by your service provider. You can find out here how to collect, read and reply to it.

## Reading an e-mail

To collect e-mail, you need to be on-line. Open your e-mail window and select the button or menu item that searches for new mail. Most programs have an icon or message that tells you when new mail arrives. Any mail will automatically be downloaded. You can then disconnect from the Net before you read it.

Many e-mail programs place new mail in a folder or in-box. When you open the folder, the messages will appear in a list detailing their sender, subject and date.

To read a message, double-click on its name in the list. It will appear, with a header section specifying its sender, subject and date, followed by the text of the message itself.

## Replying to an e-mail

Many programs make it very easy to send a reply. You simply open the message you want to reply to and select a reply button or menu item. In Netscape Mail, this button is called *Re:Mail*. A message composition window will appear, with the *Mail To:* box addressed to the sender and the *Subject:* box filled in. The body of the message will contain a copy of the original e-mail. You can delete it or edit it down to remind the sender which message you are replying to.

## Bouncing e-mail

Sometimes e-mail doesn't reach its destination. Any e-mail that fails to get through and is sent back to you is said to have "bounced". If your e-mail bounces right away, check that the address is correct. If it bounces after a couple of days, there has probably been an equipment failure on the Net. Try sending it again.

## Send yourself e-mail

To try out your e-mail program, you can send an e-mail to yourself. Put your own e-mail address in the *Mail To:* box. Alternatively, e-mail an organization called Mailbase. They will automatically send you back an e-mail. The address for America and Canada is:

**mail-server@rtfm.mit.edu**

Leave the subject line blank and enter this message in the body:
send usenet/news.answers/internet-services/access-via-email.

Mailbase's address in Europe and Asia is:

**MAILBASE@mailbase.ac.uk**

Leave the subject line blank and enter this message: send lis-iis e-access-inet.txt

## Attachments

Some e-mails that will be sent to you may include an "attachment". An attachment is a file added to an e-mail. It can be a text, a picture or a sound file.

To read an attachment you need to select a button or menu item in your e-mail window and follow the instructions you are given.

# Mailing lists

A sure way of receiving lots of e-mail is to join one of the many mailing lists available via the Net. They are correspondance groups in which you can discuss a wide variety of topics with other enthusiasts, sending and receiving articles by e-mail.

## Finding a mailing list

To find an index of the mailing lists available on the Net, open your Web browser and type in the following URL:

**http://www.Neosoft.com/internet/paml/bysubj.html**

A menu of topic groups, like the one shown below, will appear. When you click on a topic in which you are interested, you will see a list of the mailing lists related to that topic. Click on the name of a list to see a brief description of the types of issues discussed by its subscribers.

*A list of mailing lists available on the Net*

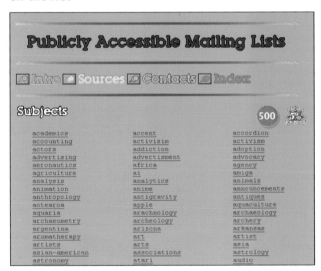

## Welcome

After you have subscribed to a mailing list, you should receive a reply to your e-mail within a few minutes or a few hours. Make sure you keep this "welcome" e-mail, as you may need to refer to it. The message will confirm you have joined successfully. It may also give you some rules of the list, the address to which you send e-mail and how to unsubscribe from the list when you want to.

Many mailing lists have administrators who oversee the messages sent in. In your welcome e-mail you may be told the e-mail address of the list administrator. You can e-mail them if you have any specific problems or questions.

## What next?

As a member of a mailing list, you will receive a copy of all the e-mails sent to the list. Download these messages in the way you would download any e-mail (see page 20).

## Subscribing to a list

The page containing a description of a mailing list should also include instructions about how to subscribe to it. Follow these instructions closely. Each mailing list has a slightly different system. It usually involves sending an e-mail to a specified address, with a specified subject line or message in the body of the e-mail.

## Sending e-mail to a list

To send a message to a mailing list, simply compose an e-mail message in the way described on pages 18 and 19. Send it to the address specified in your welcome e-mail.

Make sure you don't send any personal messages intended for the list administrator to the mailing list e-mail address by mistake.

# Newsgroups

By joining discussion groups called newsgroups, you can use the Net to get in touch with people who share the same interests as you. Most newsgroups discuss very little actual news – a lot of it is chat and trivia, but it's fun!

## Usenet newsgroups

Newsgroups form a part of the Net called Usenet. There are over 15,000 newsgroups available for you to join. Each one has a single theme, covering interests and hobbies, from jazz music to jets, from jokes to jobs.

Some newsgroups are dedicated to discussion, while others are more like helplines where you can ask questions and get advice from the experts around the world.

When you join a newsgroup, a copy of all the articles recently written by members of the group will be sent to you. You can read these articles, write your own, or join in ongoing debates.

## Newsgroup names

Each Usenet newsgroup has a unique name. The name acts as a guide to its theme. The name has two main parts. The first part describes what basic topic the group covers, such as science or computing.

The following are the abbreviations used for some of the main newsgroup topics:-

**alt.** Alternative newsgroups. These cover all kinds of topics, but usually in a humorous, crazy and alternative way.

**biz.** Business newsgroups. These cover discussions of new products, ideas and job opportunities.

**comp.** Computing newsgroups. These cover everything to do with computing and computer technology. They are great places to start looking for expert help.

**misc.** Miscellaneous newsgroups. These cover subjects such as health, kids, and books which don't fit any other topic group.

**news.** Newsgroup newsgroups. These offer tips and advice for people using Usenet for the first time.

**rec.** Recreational activities newsgroups. These cover sports, hobbies and games, from skateboarding to sewing.

**sci.** Scientific newsgroups. These are mainly used by academics to discuss their research.

**soc.** and **talk.** Social and talk newsgroups. These offer the opportunity to discuss and debate social issues, different cultures, politics, religion and philosophy.

The second part of a newsgroup name, known as its subtopics, narrows down the topic area the group concerns. For example, an imaginary newsgroup name might be **rec.music.presley**. This tells you that the newsgroup is in the recreational activities topic group. Its subtopic is music, more specifically the music of Elvis Presley.

## Newsgroup access

Most access providers will give you access to Usenet newsgroups as part of your Internet package. They should supply you with a program called a newsreader, which enables you to read and send newsgroup articles.

Some browsers, such as Netscape Navigator, include a newsreader facility. For this, you will need to open a special newsreader window.

## Opening your newsreader

Once you are on-line, open your newsreader window. First you need to display a list of the names of all the newsgroups available. To do this, select the button or menu item which invites you to view all newsgroups. A list like the one below will appear. The newsreader window shown below is Netscape News from Netscape Navigator 2.01.

You need to be on-line so that you can look at this list. Your computer will download it from a computer called a news server. Once it has been downloaded, you can disconnect while you look at it.

## Choosing a newsgroup

Scroll through the list of newsgroup topics, opening topic folders to see which subtopics they contain. If, for example, you wanted to find a group that discussed mountain biking, you would click on **rec.\*** to see a list of its subtopics. Next you would click on **rec.bicycles** and, finally, on **rec.bicycles.offroad**.

## Subscribing

To subscribe to a newsgroup, simply locate its name in the list and select a subscribe button or menu item. In the Netscape News window you click in the box beside the group's name. You don't have to pay to join a Usenet newsgroup.

## Unsubscribing

To unsubscribe from a newsgroup, click in the box so that the check mark disappears, or select an unsubscribe button or menu item.

*A list of newsgroups in a section of the Netscape News window*

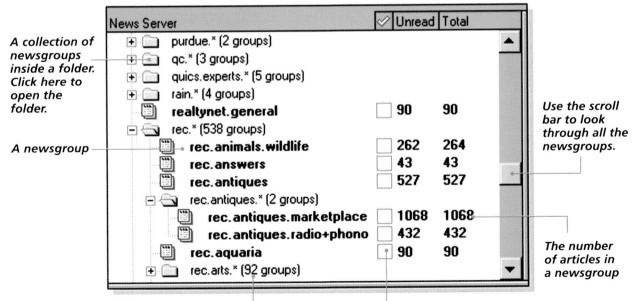

*A collection of newsgroups inside a folder. Click here to open the folder.*

*A newsgroup*

| News Server | | Unread | Total |
|---|---|---|---|
| ⊞ 📁 purdue.* (2 groups) | | | |
| ⊞ 📁 qc.* (3 groups) | | | |
| ⊞ 📁 quics.experts.* (5 groups) | | | |
| ⊞ 📁 rain.* (4 groups) | | | |
| 📄 **realtynet.general** | | 90 | 90 |
| ⊟ 📂 rec.* (538 groups) | | | |
| 📄 **rec.animals.wildlife** | | 262 | 264 |
| 📄 **rec.answers** | | 43 | 43 |
| 📄 **rec.antiques** | | 527 | 527 |
| ⊟ 📂 rec.antiques.* (2 groups) | | | |
| 📄 **rec.antiques.marketplace** | | 1068 | 1068 |
| 📄 **rec.antiques.radio+phono** | | 432 | 432 |
| 📄 **rec.aquaria** | | 90 | 90 |
| ⊞ 📁 rec.arts.* (92 groups) | | | |

*Use the scroll bar to look through all the newsgroups.*

*The number of articles in a newsgroup*

*This number tells you how many newsgroups this topic group contains.*

*A mark will appear in this box when you join or subscribe to this group.*

# Posting to newsgroups

As a new member of a newsgroup, you'll be known as a newbie. It's fun to get involved in debates and discussions or ask for information and advice. On these pages you'll find out how to join in by receiving and sending newsgroup articles.

## Collecting articles

Messages sent to newsgroups are called articles or postings. Once you have subscribed to a newsgroup, a computer called a news server will send you a copy of all the articles that have recently been posted to that group.

To collect these articles, you need to be on-line. Open your newsreader window. A number will appear beside the name of each of the newsgroups you belong to. This number indicates how many new articles are currently available in the newsgroup.

## Reading articles

Click on the name of the newsgroup that you want to look at. A list of all the new articles in it will appear. Click on the name of an article to download it.

You should disconnect from the Net before you read articles, because you don't want to pay for a long telephone connection.

## Keeping track

Once you have read an article, your newsreader will mark it as "read". This means that the next time you come back to the newsgroup you won't see that message. This ensures that only new articles you haven't read before are displayed in the list.

Check regularly to see if you have received anything from your newsgroup, because most news servers delete articles after a few days.

**This is the Netscape News window showing an article open.**

**Number of articles currently in each newsgroup**

**A list of the newsgroups to which the user is subscribed**

**Click here to see the articles in this newsgroup.**

**A list of articles in the alt.cybercafes newsgroup**

**Click to open an article.**

**This article has already been read.**

**The text of an article**

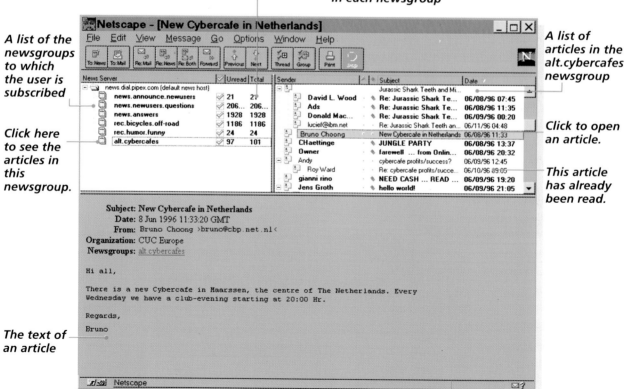

## Lurking

When you first join a newsgroup, don't start posting articles right away. Spend a couple of days reading the ones written by other members first, to get an idea of what kind of discussions are currently in progress. This is called lurking.

## Frequently Asked Questions

Most newsgroups have a Frequently Asked Question (FAQ) article. This is a list of the questions most often asked by new members. It saves other members from having to answer the same questions again and again. The FAQ article will appear every couple of weeks. Read it before you start posting.

## Ready to post

When you post an article to a newsgroup, you have three options: you can start a new discussion, join in an existing one, or e-mail (see page 17) a personal response to someone else's article. Starting a new discussion is known as starting a new thread. To do this, open your newsreader window. Click on the name of the newsgroup to which you want to send your article. Click the *To: News* button. A message composition window will appear.

**Compose your article in a message window.**

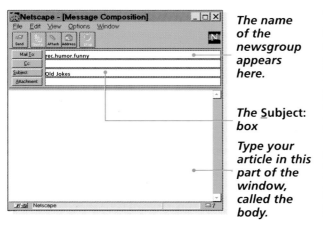

*The name of the newsgroup appears here.*

*The Subject: box*

*Type your article in this part of the window, called the body.*

Summarize the contents of your article in the *Subject:* box, so that people scanning through the list of articles will know if your article will interest them. Write your article in the area of the composition window called the body. For some advice on writing articles, see page 26.

When your article is ready, connect to the Net and select the send button or menu item.

## Responding

There are two ways in which you can respond to an existing article. The first is by sending a reply to the newsgroup. This is known as following up. The second is by responding personally to the author of an article by sending them an e-mail. This is called replying.

Open the article you want to respond to. To follow up, select *Re:News*. To reply personally by e-mail select *Re:Mail*. (It is considered good manners to send an e-mail to the author of an article you are following up. To do this, press *Re:Both*.)

A window will appear in which you can type your message. The *Mail To:* box will automatically be addressed and the body of the message will contain a copy of the article to which you are responding. Edit it down to the points your article is answering.

Compose your message, connect to the Net, and then select the send button or menu item.

### ✉ Getting advice

You can join a newsgroup called **news.announce.newusers** for advice on using Usenet newsgroups.

If you want to check that you are posting articles correctly, you can send a message to **misc.test**. You will automatically get a reply to your message a few days later.

# Netiquette

There aren't many rules about what you can and can't do on the Net, but there are things that are considered good and bad manners. Users have developed a code of conduct known as Netiquette. Here are some rules to follow when composing articles for newsgroups or sending e-mail.

## Keep it brief

Make sure everything you write is brief and to the point. Express yourself as clearly and concisely as you can. People have to download your articles, and the longer they are, the more time and money they will cost to download.

## Watch your tone

When you are talking with someone on the telephone, it's easy to know whether they are being funny or sarcastic by the tone of their voice. When typing a message, however, it's hard to show emotion. Some Net users put words in brackets to indicate their state of mind, such as <grin> or <sob>.

Another way of showing emotion on the Net is to use little pictures called smileys or emoticons. They are made up of keyboard characters and when you look at them sideways they are like faces. New smileys are being made up all the time. Here are some useful ones.

| | | | |
|---|---|---|---|
| :-D | Laughing | :-P | Tongue out |
| :-( | Sad/angry | :-/ | Confused |
| :-) | Happy/sarcastic | :* | Kissing |
| :-X | Not saying a word | 0:-) | Angel |
| :-O | Wow! | $-) | Greedy |
| :*) | Clowning around | :-I | Grim |
| I-O | Bored | :'-) | Crying |

## Use an acronym

To avoid too much typing, some Net users have taken to using "acronyms", which are abbreviations of familiar phrases. They usually use the first letter of each word. Here are some of the most commonly used acronyms:

| | |
|---|---|
| BTW | By The Way |
| DL | DownLoad |
| FYI | For Your Information |
| IMHO | In My Humble Opinion |
| OTT | Over The Top |
| POV | Point Of View |
| TIA | Thanks In Advance |
| TTFN | Ta Ta For Now |
| UL | UpLoad |
| WRT | With Reference To |

## No shouting and flaming

When you type a message, don't use UPPER CASE letters, because in Net speak this is the equivalent of shouting. It is considered rude and will annoy your fellow Net users. If you break the code of Netiquette or post an article that makes someone angry, you will get "flamed". This means that you will receive lots of angry messages, known as flame mail, from other users.

## No spamming

Spamming is Internet slang for sending a huge number of useless or rude messages to a single person or site. The word is also used to describe a technique used by certain businesses which send messages advertising their products to thousands of different users via the Net.

# The World Wide Web

The World Wide Web, also known as the Web or WWW, is probably the most exciting part of the Net. Art galleries, magazines, music samples, sports, games, educational material and movie previews are all available on the Web. It's not only interesting, but it's easy to use too.

## Web pages

The Web is made up of millions of documents called Web pages. You will see a selection of the kinds of information they contain on pages 28 and 29. Web pages are stored on different computers all over the world. A computer on which Web pages are stored is called a host or server.

## Browsers

To look at Web pages, you need a browser (see page 12). If you have the Microsoft® Windows® 95, Macintosh System 7 or OS/2 Warp operating systems you will probably already have a browser. The software provided by an access provider should include a browser.

## Starting your browser

To start your browser, connect up to the Net and select the Web button or menu item in your menu window. Your browser window will open. The window shown below is Netscape Navigator 4.0. Most browsers will have similar features.

When you launch your browser, a Web page may automatically appear in its window. This page is known as the default page and usually contains information about the manufacturer of the browser.

The default page will not appear in the browser window immediately, because it takes some time to send Web pages over the Net. For a few minutes the central part of your browser window will remain blank.

*The Netscape Navigator browser window*

**The Home button - Click here to come back to your chosen default page.**

**The name of the Web page**

**The browser's tool bar**

**This location box contains the name of the page currently displayed.**

**This picture moves while the browser is searching for Web pages.**

**The window in which the pages are displayed.**

**This box displays information about what the browser is doing.**

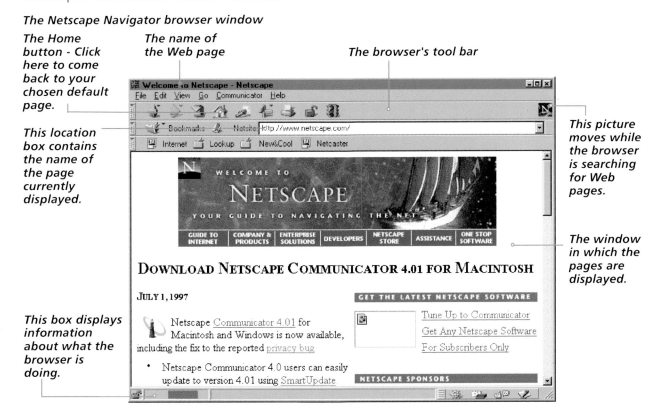

# Web pages

The information on the Web can be presented in a variety of ways. Web pages may contain words or pictures, or more exciting ways of presenting information, such as video clips. Many Web pages are "multimedia" documents. This means two or more methods of presenting information have been combined in a single page. So a page with both pictures and sounds is an example of multimedia.

This section shows some of the kinds of pages that are on the Web, and some of the ways in which the information is presented.

## Video and animation

Some pages contain moving images. For example, you can watch extracts from movies and clips from music videos. Short animation sequences are sometimes added to Web pages to make them more exciting.

## Up-to-date information

Web pages can be updated regularly, so they are particularly useful for displaying news, weather forecasts and sports results. Web pages may contain charts and graphs which continually update themselves according to the latest statistics. You can also find travel information, such as train and plane times, on the Web.

## Software

There are many Web pages that tell you where to find software on the Internet. A wide variety of programs are available for you to copy onto your computer. Some of them are free, others you have to pay for. Many of the programs help you to enjoy the Web more, by allowing you to watch the videos and listen to the music included on some pages.

## Music and sound

Web pages can contain sounds, such as recordings of famous speeches or sound effects. There are Web pages devoted to different types of music, from classical to country, and punk to pop. Some of these pages include music clips to listen to.

## Personal pages

Many people create Web pages to share information about themselves or their interests with other Web users. Some personal pages contain photographs of the people who wrote them, their friends and their families.

## Pictures

You can find a variety of pictures on the Web. Pictures created using a computer, called computer graphics, photographs, maps and diagrams are often used to illustrate factual information and stories. Some Web pages contain only pictures. You can find photographs of places, wildlife, famous people, and works of art.

## Bigger and better

The Web is a very popular part of the Internet. More and more people and organizations are adding their own pages to it every day. As a result, the Web is growing rapidly. The information is frequently updated, and improvements in technology allow people to present it in new and exciting ways.

# Finding Web pages

The Web is made up of millions of pages of information. Despite its vast size, it's easy to find your way around, because every page has an address and all the pages are interlinked.

## Web addresses

The addresses given to pieces of information on the Net, such as Web pages, are called URLs (Uniform Resource Locators). They may look complicated, but they are simple to understand.

The imaginary URL below shows the three main parts of an address:

**http://www.usborne.co.uk/public/homepage.htm**

The first part, the "protocol name", specifies the type of document the page is. **http://** tells you that the page is a Web page. Some pieces of information have different protocol names, such as **ftp://** (see page 44).

**http://www.usborne.co.uk/public/homepage.htm**

The second part, the "host name", is the name of the computer on which the page is stored.

**http://www.usborne.co.uk/public/homepage.htm**

The final part, the "file path", specifies the file in which the page is stored and the name of the directory in which that file can be found.

The URL shown above tells you that the page is a Web page. It is stored on a site belonging to a company called Usborne in the UK. The file containing the page is called homepage.htm, which is found in a directory called public.

### ⚠ Be careful

When you write down or type a URL, make sure that you copy it exactly. There are no spaces between letters. Take note of where upper case letters are used and where lower case letters are used.

## Finding a Web page

To find a particular Web page for which you have a URL, you need to be on-line. Type the URL into your browser's window and press the Return key. In Netscape Navigator you type the URL into a box, known as the location box.

When a page appears in your browser window it is said to have been "downloaded". This means that its contents have been stored in your computer's temporary memory. Even if you disconnect from the Net, you'll still be able to see the page.

## Give it a try

Try typing in the following Web address so that you can have a closer look at a Web page:
**http://www.nasa.gov/**.
A Web page created by the National Aeronautics and Space Administation (NASA) will appear in your browser's window.

*Type the URL in this box.*

*The Netscape logo moves while the browser is downloading a page.*

*This box indicates the size of an incoming page, how much of it has been downloaded and when downloading is complete.*

*Use the scroll bars to view the whole page.*

## Hyperlinks

It is very easy to move around the Web because Web pages are interconnected. They contain words or pictures which link them to other Web pages containing related information. These words and pictures are known as hyperlinks.

When you point to a hyperlink on a page, your pointer changes into a hand symbol like this. If you click with your mouse on the link, a new page will be automatically downloaded onto your computer. The link may take you to another page on the same site or to a site somewhere else on the Net.

When you point at a hyperlink, the URL of the page to which you will be transferred is displayed somewhere in your browser window.

Words which are hyperlinks can also be called hypertext. They are usually underlined or highlighted. Hyperlink pictures may be photographs or computer graphics. Some hyperlink computer graphics look like buttons. Others are small pictures which represent the page to which the hyperlink connects.

The picture below shows how you can use hyperlinks to jump between pages.

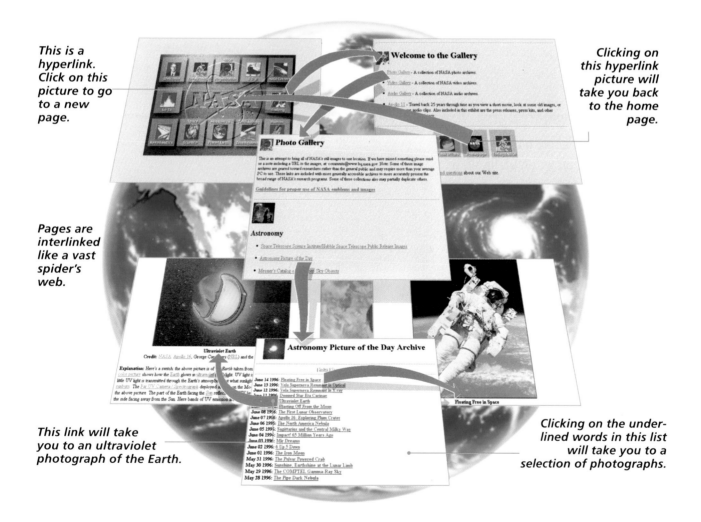

*This is a hyperlink. Click on this picture to go to a new page.*

*Clicking on this hyperlink picture will take you back to the home page.*

*Pages are interlinked like a vast spider's web.*

*This link will take you to an ultraviolet photograph of the Earth.*

*Clicking on the underlined words in this list will take you to a selection of photographs.*

# Browsing the Web

In this section you can find out some ways to save time and effort when exploring or "browsing" the Web.

## Finding your way

It is easy to get lost when you are browsing the Web. You can get carried away following hyperlinks. Don't worry. Your browser automatically records which pages you have looked at during a browsing session.

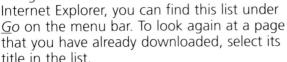

Most browsers can show you a list of these pages. In both Netscape Navigator and Microsoft Internet Explorer, you can find this list under Go on the menu bar. To look again at a page that you have already downloaded, select its title in the list.

Most browsers also have buttons on the tool bar that you can use to retrace your steps. The examples shown below are from Netscape Navigator. Don't worry if you have a different browser; other browsers have tool bar buttons with very similar pictures or names.

 The Back button instructs your browser to show the page you looked at before the one it is currently displaying.

 Once you have moved back, you can use the Forward button. This tells your browser to show the page that you originally saw after the one you are currently looking at.

 The Home button on your browser's tool bar takes you back to your browser's default page.
You can find out how to choose a different default page on page 48.

## A second look

When you look at a page for a second time during a browsing session, the page appears in your browser window almost immediately. This is because your browser displays the copy of the page that it stored in your computer's memory. You don't have to wait for the page to be sent over the Internet again.

You can use the Reload or Refresh button to instruct your browser to ignore the copy of a Web page which is stored in your computer's memory, and to download another copy from the Internet. This is useful when you are looking at a page that contains information which changes frequently, for example, a page displaying sports results.

## Web sites

A group of Web pages created by a person or an organization is called a Web site. The pages that make up a Web site are usually stored on the same host computer.

The main page of a Web site is called its home page. It usually tells you what you will find on the site, although it may not be the first page you see when you visit a site.

To help you to explore a Web site without getting lost, the pages that make up the site usually contain a hyperlink to the site's home page. This may appear as an icon, a button, or the word home.

**This is the hyperlink that links pages on the LEGO Web site to its home page.**

Don't confuse a home page hyperlink on a Web page with the Home button on your browser's tool bar.

## Saving time

Some Web pages, especially those which contain pictures, take a long time to download. To save time, you can download the text on its own. Here's how you can instruct your browser to leave out the pictures.

 Select *Preferences...* from the *Edit* menu. A dialog box will appear on your screen. Choose *Advanced* from the directory tree on the left, then look at the check boxes on the right. If there is a mark next to the *Automatically load images* item, your browser will automatically download pictures. Make sure this item is not selected.

 Choose *Options* from the *View* menu. A dialog box will appear on your screen. On the *General* form, make sure that *Show pictures* is not selected.

When your browser downloads a text-only version of a Web page, it replaces the pictures with small icons.

**This is the icon that Netscape Navigator uses to replace pictures.**

If you decide that you want to see an image, click on the icon that replaces it, and your browser will download the picture.

## Stop

You may start downloading a page which turns out to be uninteresting or offensive. You can stop downloading a page at any time by clicking the *Stop* button on your browser.

 Once you have pressed the *Stop* button, wait for your browser to respond. This may take a few seconds because your browser has to contact the host computer to cancel the downloading process. Don't keep clicking the *Stop* button or pressing the Return key. This will stop your browser from working temporarily and may even crash your computer.

## Rush hour

If a lot of people are using the Net at the same time as you are, it may take a long time to download Web pages.

The Internet is like a road. When there is a lot of traffic on a road, the vehicles move more slowly than when there is only a little traffic. In the same way, the more people there are sending and receiving data over the Net, the slower the information travels.

If you want to get more done during the time you spend on-line, try using the Net late at night or early in the morning. You may find it is less busy.

## Surfing in cyberspace

In Internet slang "surfing the Net" means exploring the Internet, looking for interesting things to do. Some people say that this comes from the expression "channel surfing", which means rapidly changing television channels at random, looking for interesting programs.

A channel surfer switches between television channels just as a surfer catches one wave and then another. Similarly, a "Net surfer" moves around the Internet, jumping from one file to another.

When you surf the Net and browse the Web, you physically stay in one place. However, you make an imaginary journey across the world by linking up to computers in different places. The name of the imaginary space that you travel through is cyberspace.

# Gathering information

You may come across information on the Web that you want to look at again and again. You can either create short cuts to these Web pages or save the information onto disk.

## Hotlists

A "hotlist" is a collection of short cuts to Web pages that you want to look at regularly. It's called a hotlist because "hot" is slang for something that is good or popular. The short cuts allow you to download particular Web pages without having to remember their URLs.

To add a page to a hotlist, display the page in your browser window, then follow the instructions below.

 In Netscape Navigator, the hotlist is called "Bookmarks". Select *Bookmarks* from the *Communicator* menu to make the *Bookmarks* menu appear. Then choose *Add Bookmark* from the *Bookmarks* menu.

 Microsoft Internet Explorer calls its hotlist "Favorites". Select *Add to Favorites...* from the *Favorites...* menu. A box may appear asking you to confirm your choice.

## Using hotlists

To instruct your browser to download a page from your hotlist, follow the instructions below.

 You can find a list of your bookmarks in the *Bookmarks* menu. Click on the name of the Web page that you want to see, and your browser will download it.

 The *Favorites...* menu contains a list of short cuts to Web pages. Click on the name of the Web page that you want your browser to display.

To make it easier to find your short cuts, you can arrange them into folders. Click on *Edit Bookmarks...* or *Organize Favorites...* to display your hotlist window, then use the buttons or menus to create folders. To move a short cut into a folder, simply drag it to a new location.

*Microsoft Internet Explorer's hotlist*

*Select a Web page from the list to download it.*

## Saving information

The Web is changing all the time. The URLs of some pages change and other pages are removed from the Web altogether. You may want to save some information into your computer's permanent memory or onto floppy disks so that you can look at it again later.

> ### ⚠ Copyright
>
> Most of the information on the Web is available free. This doesn't mean that you can do what you like with it. If you want to publish either pictures or text in any way, (including elsewhere on the Web), you must first obtain permission from the person or company that owns the copyright. If you don't do this, you may be breaking the law. It is okay to save information onto your computer for personal use without asking.

## Saving text

To save the text from a Web page that is displayed in your browser window, select *Save As...* from the *File* menu. Use the *Save As...* dialog box to give the page a filename and to instruct your computer where to save it.

### The Save As... dialog box

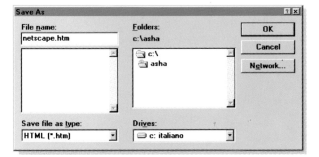

You must also choose how to save the page. Select one of the options listed under *Save as type*. When you save as *HTML*, the Web page keeps the same layout, but icons appear instead of pictures. If you select *Plain Text*, the copy you make will look very different from the Web page. For example, there will be no pictures and a different lettering and layout style will be used.

### The Garfield page on the Web

**The Garfield page saved as HTML**

**The same page saved as Plain Text**

*Pictures saved from:*
*http://www.pdimages.com/*

## Saving pictures

When you save a Web page, you have to save each picture on it separately. To save a picture, point at it with your mouse and press your mouse button down. (If you are using a PC, use the right button.) Select the item called *Save Image as...* (or something similar) from the menu which appears. Use the *Save As...* dialog box to choose a name and location for the picture.

## Saving links

You can use a hyperlink to save a Web page without actually displaying the page in your browser window.

For example, you may want to save a selection of pages from a Web site that you have explored in a previous browsing session. Download the home page. You can now save other pages on that site using the hyperlinks which appear on the home page. Click on a hyperlink with your mouse and select *Save Link as* from the pop-up menu. Then use the *Save As...* dialog box as before.

## Viewing saved information

You can look at any text and pictures you have saved when you are off-line. Launch your browser without connecting to the Net, then select *Open...* or *Open Page...* from the *File* menu. To display the *Open* dialog box, click on the *Browse...* or *Choose File...* button. Then use the dialog box in the usual way to find and select the file you want to see. If the file you are looking for isn't listed, change the entry under *Files of type* to *All Files*.

# *Searching the Web*

You may need to use the Web to find out something specific, for example, for a school project. It can be hard to do this by clicking on hyperlinks at random. There are several programs on the Web, known as search services, that will help you find what you are looking for.

## Search services

There are two types of search services: search engines (see pages 38 to 41) and directories. Directories are huge lists of hyperlinks to Web pages. The hyperlinks are organized into various categories according to the content of the pages they link to. For example, you will find hyperlinks to pages about music under the category "Entertainment".

## Finding search services

Some browsers have a button which will lead you to a Web page containing a list of several different search services.

If your browser doesn't have this facility, you can find the URLs of search services in Internet magazines.

Here are the URLs of three useful directories:
Lycos at **http://a2z.lycos.com/**
Infoseek at **http://www.infoseek.com/**
Yahoo! at **http://www.yahoo.com/**.
It is a good idea to add them to your hotlist (see page 34).

## Directory levels

Yahoo! is a popular directory.

Its home page has 14 large subject areas for you to choose from, including Computers and Internet, Society and Culture and Health. These are hyperlinks. When you click on one, you move down to another level of the directory, where there are smaller subject areas.

Clicking on one of these takes you to yet another level, with even smaller subject areas. This process of narrowing down the subject area is known as drilling down.

## Using a directory

Say, for example, you want to use Yahoo! to find some pages containing information about natural history museums. On the home page, click on Society and Culture. A page will appear containing several categories which are all related to society and culture, including Museums and Exhibits.

Follow the Museums and Exhibits link. On the next level there are more options, for example Art, Science, and Natural History. When you click on the Natural History hyperlink, you will be presented with a list of hyperlinks to the home pages of natural history museums all over the world.

*Using the Yahoo! directory to find natural history museums*

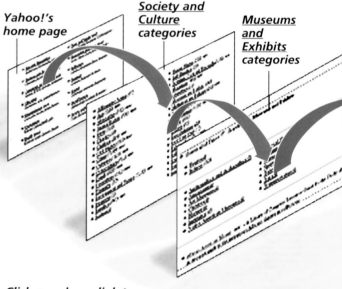

Yahoo!'s home page

**Society and Culture categories**

**Museums and Exhibits categories**

*Click on a hyperlink to move down a level.*

*As you move through the directory levels, the subject areas become narrower.*

## Categories

Directories are compiled by people called editors who look at Web pages and decide which category each page should go in.

It may take you some time to get used to the way the pages in a directory are grouped together. Some topics fit naturally in more than one group. For example, pages about medicines could go under <u>Health</u> or <u>Science</u>.

When searching for information about a particular subject, it is a good idea to try all the possible categories in which it might be included.

## Incomplete lists

Directories are not complete lists of all the pages on the Web. The Web is growing so rapidly that it is impossible for the editors of directories to classify all the new pages.

Editors have different methods of discovering Web pages to include in their lists. Many of them use computer programs to find pages which have recently been added to the Web.

Each directory is a unique selection of Web pages. If you can't find any information about a subject in one directory, you may find it in another one.

## Web chaos

Search services are extremely useful because the Web is a very disorganized place. Nobody owns the Web and nobody controls it. Anyone can create a Web page or site without having to tell a central organization what information it contains or where it can be found.

Imagine a library where people were allowed to bring any book and place it wherever they wanted to, on the shelves or on the floor. It would be difficult to find a particular book. The Web is as chaotic as this imaginary library would be.

### ⚠ Missing pages

Directories are so huge that it is difficult for editors to keep checking that the URLs listed are still correct. You may find a hyperlink in a directory which doesn't work, either because the page has been moved to another server, or because it has been removed from the Web altogether. When this happens, an error message will appear on your screen.

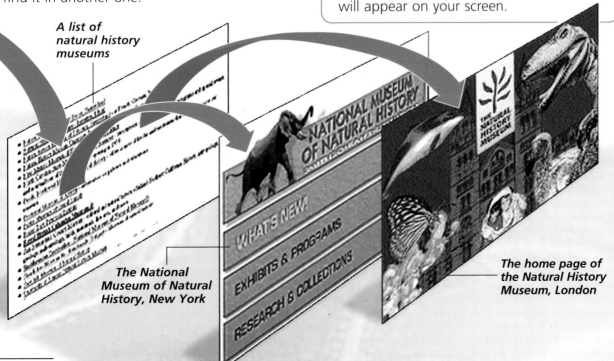

*A list of natural history museums*

*The National Museum of Natural History, New York*

*The home page of the Natural History Museum, London*

# Word searches

Some search services allow you to search the Web for pages which contain particular words. They are known as search engines, or search indexes.

## Key words

The "key words" of a Web page are the words which sum up its contents. For example, the key words of a Web page that explains what turtles eat are *turtles*, *food* and *eat*.

When you instruct a search engine to look for key words, it looks through an index of millions of Web pages that it has compiled. Any page the search engine finds which contains the word or words you require is known as a hit. The search engine will present the results of its search in a list. This may be one or several pages long, depending on how many hits there are.

## Finding search engines

Here are the URLs of some useful search engines:
AltaVista at **http://www.altavista.digital.com/**
Open Text at **http://www.opentext.com/**
Webcrawler at **http://webcrawler.com/**
HotBot at **http://www.hotbot.com/**.

## Simple searches

Say, for example, you wanted to use the AltaVista search engine to

find out about turtles. Go to the AltaVista home page. You will see a blank strip known as a query box like the one shown here.

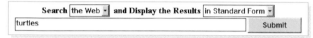

This is where you enter the key words. To do this, click in the space with your mouse, then type **turtles**. Next, click on the button which instructs the search engine to start the search. AltaVista calls this button *Submit*, but other search engines have a different names for it, such as *Search* or *Go Get It*.

After a few seconds, the search engine will produce a list of hits. Each item in the list includes a hyperlink to a Web page which contains the key word, and a short description of that page. This will help you decide which of the pages in the list is likely to be the most suitable. When you find an interesting-looking hyperlink, click on it to download the page.

*A selection of the hits that AltaVista found for the word turtle*

*A results page*

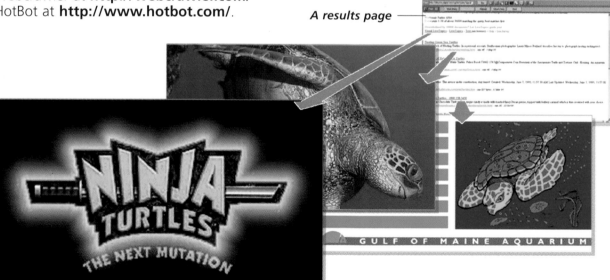

## Expert searching

Sometimes results pages will contain thousands and thousands of entries. Many of these will have nothing to do with the subject you are interested in. For example, if you carry out a key word search on the word **rock**, the hits will include pages about music and about geology.

You can use a selection of words or symbols, known as operators, to give the search engine more precise instructions. This will reduce the chances of it turning up pages that don't interest you.

Check the instructions of a search engine to see whether you should use words or symbols. Some search engines have pull down menus from which you select the appropriate operator. With others, you have to type the operator into the query box.

## Using operators

Here are some widely used operators:

 To make your instructions more specific, you can say you want two or more words to appear on the Web page. Type a plus sign before each word, or the word AND between the words. For example, if you want to find pages about rock music, you would type **+rock +music** or **rock AND music**.

You can also tell a search engine which words you don't want to appear on the page. Type a minus sign or the word NOT before any words you wish to avoid. For example, to find pages about any styles of music except jazz and classical, you would enter **music -jazz -classical** or **music NOT jazz NOT classical**.

If you enter more than one word in the query box without any operators, it usually makes the instruction less precise. Most search engines will look for pages which contain any of the words, and will find even more hits.

## Spelling

Search engines look for the exact word or words you enter in the query box. It is very important, therefore, to make sure that you spell the word correctly. If you don't, you may find that there are no hits.

Search engines are usually "case-insensitive". This means that they don't distinguish between capital (upper case) letters or small (lower case) letters. So it doesn't matter which kind of letters you use when you type key words into a query box.

## Creepy-crawlies

Search engines use special software to create their indexes. Each search engine has its own program that automatically builds up the index. The program constantly crawls across the Web, collecting information about Web pages. It also sorts the data into categories, and adds it to the index.

Some search engines are called crawlers, spiders or worms. These names refer to the different types of programs that the various search engines use to collect data about Web pages.

# Expert searching

Here are some tips on how to make a search engine find exactly what you are looking for.

## Phrases

You can instruct some search engines to search for pages where a group of words appear in a particular order.

AltaVista and WebCrawler will search for phrases if you enclose the words in quotation marks. For example, to find some Web pages about the Leaning Tower of Pisa, click with your mouse in a query box and type **"the Leaning Tower of Pisa"**.

You can also search for phrases using the Open Text search engine. You don't have to enclose the words in quotation marks. Instead, select *this exact phrase* from the drop-down menu to the left of the query box.

*There are many pictures of the Leaning Tower of Pisa, Italy, on the Web.*

## Wild card

A search engine looks for the exact words you type into its query box. So when a search engine is looking for the word musician, it will not turn up pages that contain similar words such as music and musicians.

Some search engines, however, allow you to replace the different beginnings or endings of a word with a little star, called an asterisk. This symbol is often called the wild card. So, for example, if you type **music\*** into a query box, this tells a search engine to look for any words which begin with music.

## Searching by date

AltaVista can perform an "advanced" search. This means you can give it very specific instructions about the information you require. For example, you can use AltaVista to search for pages according to when they were put on the Web, or when the information on a page last changed. This is especially useful when you only want to find up-to-date information on a particular subject.

Say, for example, you wanted to use AltaVista to find information about fashion which was added to the Web over the last month. You would need to use AltaVista's advanced query form. To see this form, click on the *Advanced Search* button on the AltaVista home page.

*AltaVista's advanced query form*

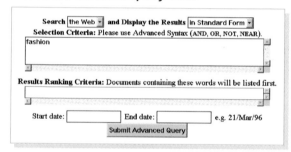

At the bottom of the form there are two boxes called *Start date:* and *End date:*. Enter whatever the date was one month ago in the first box, and today's date in the second box. Click on *Submit Advanced Query* to start the search.

*Pictures from a fashion site found by AltaVista*

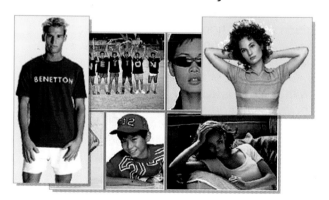

# Search results

You can often choose how you want the results of a search to be displayed. For example, you may be able to decide how many hits you want to see listed at a time, and how much information about them you want included on the results page.

## Number of hits

Most search engines show 10 hyperlinks on each results page. So, a search which found 100 hits would produce 10 pages of results.

You can change the number of links you want to see. WebCrawler, for example, can display either 10, 25 or 100 results per page. On its home page, select the number you prefer from the drop-down menu which is located above the query box.

*The WebCrawler query box*

**Select how many links you want to see on each results page here.**

Each search engine works in a slightly different way, but most of them have similar drop-down menus on their home pages.

## Descriptions

Search engines usually let you choose how much information you want to read about each hyperlink on their results pages. A description can range from a few words to a long paragraph.

WebCrawler, for example, allows you to choose between seeing only the titles of Web pages, or reading summaries of their contents. Select the option you prefer from a drop-down menu on its home page.

## Order

Search engines present the results of a key word search in a particular order. The hits which best match your requirements appear on the first results page.

Search engines use different methods to decide which are the best matches. Some count how many times a key word appears on the page, others look at how near the key word is to the top of the page.

## Changing the order

You may find that the hits that a search engine presents first are not the ones that interest you the most. When you perform an advanced search with AltaVista, you can decide which hits it should present first.

Say, for example, you want to find out about toys and games, but you are particularly interested in games. On the AltaVista advanced query form, enter **toys OR games** into the *Selection Criteria* box. Then type **games** into the *Results Ranking Criteria* box. AltaVista considers the word you type into this box to be the most important key word.

The search engine places the hyperlinks which lead to pages about games at the top of the results page. Links to pages about toys will appear farther down the results page.

**One of the pages about toys found by AltaVista**

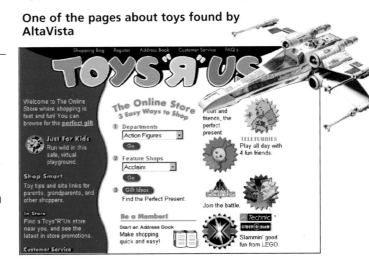

# Giving your opinion

This section shows two ways in which you can give your opinion about the sort of Web pages you want to see.

## Personalized searches

You can personalize some search services so that they only list Web pages that they know you will find interesting. The Yahoo! search service can be personalized in this way.

To create your own version of Yahoo! go to: **http://edit.my.yahoo.com/config/login/**.

## Creating your Yahoo!

Click on the *START YOUR OWN* button, then follow the on-screen instructions. You will have to complete two forms.

The first form asks you to invent a "login" name and a password. These allow Yahoo! to identify you when you use it. Both the login name and the password can be any combination of letters and numbers. It is a good idea to choose something you can remember easily, such as your name.

You will also have to provide personal information, such as your date of birth and your occupation. Enter the information required in the appropriate boxes, then click on *Register me now!* to continue.

The second form asks for information about your interests and preferences. Select the categories that interest you from the lists. Then click on *Use these interests*.

**Select interesting categories on the second form**

Click on a box with your mouse.

## Your Yahoo!

The next page to appear explains what your personalized My Yahoo! contains and what the My Yahoo! icons represent. It's a good idea to save this page so you can refer to it whenever you need to (see page 34).

To see your personalized version of Yahoo! for the first time, click on the *Take me to My Yahoo!* button.

**A personalized Yahoo page**

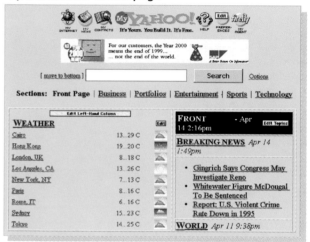

Your Yahoo! includes news pages, containing frequently updated news stories. The content  of these pages depends on the categories that you selected on the second form. For example, if you selected Technology, you might find reports about new inventions on your personalized news pages.

 You will also find a unique search page called *My Internet*. This contains Web page recommendations and short cuts to your chosen Yahoo! directory categories.

## Edit buttons

My Yahoo! contains several *Edit* buttons. You can use these to change the information you supplied when creating your Yahoo! To change any of the information that you entered on the first form, click on the *Edit* button which appears at the top of every page.

## Logging in

The next time you want to see your Yahoo! pages, go to:
**http://edit.my.yahoo.com/config/login/**.
   Enter your login name and password in the space available, then click on the *Login* button. This instructs your browser to display your Yahoo!.

## Intelligent Agents

Your Yahoo! includes an "intelligent agent" (IA). This is a special program which can learn about your likes and dislikes and find sites that are likely to interest you. Intelligent agents are often compared to dogs, because they track down Web sites on behalf of their master.

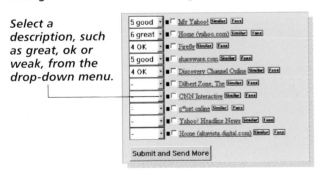

## Training

Before you can use an IA, it has to be "trained" to judge pages on your behalf. To start training your Yahoo! agent, click on the *Firefly* icon. You will have to "rate" or tell your agent what you think of at least 20 Web sites.

**Rating sites to train a Yahoo! agent**

*Select a description, such as great, ok or weak, from the drop-down menu.*

| | |
|---|---|
| 5 good | My Yahoo! Similar Fans |
| 6 great | Home (yahoo.com) Similar Fans |
| 4 OK | Firefly Similar Fans |
| 5 good | shareware.com Similar Fans |
| 4 OK | Discovery Channel Online Similar Fans |
| - | Dilbert Zone, The Similar Fans |
| | CNN Interactive Similar Fans |
| | c*net online Similar Fans |
| | Yahoo! Headline News Similar Fans |
| | Home (altavista digital com) Similar Fans |

Submit and Send More

When you have rated 20 sites, your agent will know more about what you like and dislike. It will then recommend Web sites to you. You can rate more than 20 sites if you want to. The more you train an IA, the more likely it is to recommend sites you will like.

## Sending messages

Some Web sites contain a piece of hypertext which says comment, feedback, write to us or something similar. This means that the person who looks after the site, called the Webmaster, wants to receive comments and questions from the people who have visited the site.
   When you click on the hyperlink, your browser will download a Web page containing a form similar to the one shown below. You can use this form to send a message to the Webmaster.
   You may be asked to provide some personal information, such as your name and your e-mail address (see below).
   Type your message into the main section of the form, then click on the *Send* or *Submit* button. Your message will be sent across the Internet to the Webmaster's computer.

**A message form**

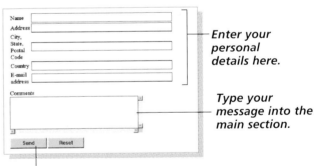

*Enter your personal details here.*

*Type your message into the main section.*

**Click here to send your message.**

## E-mail

The process of sending messages from one computer to another is called electronic mail or e-mail. Everyone who is on the Internet has a unique address to which you can send messages. You can find out more about e-mail on pages 17-21 of this book.

# Downloading programs

You can use the Web to copy software from the Internet onto your computer. Software is usually downloaded using a method called File Transfer Protocol (FTP).

## FTP and the Web

FTP is the main way of sending files over the Net. Anything which can be stored on a computer – including pictures, sound clips, text files, and software – can be transferred by FTP. The files are stored on servers all over the world, called FTP sites. The URLs of FTP sites begin with **ftp://**.

Although FTP is a separate Internet facility from the Web, a Web page can contain a direct link to a file stored on an FTP site.

## Finding programs on the Web

You can obtain a different browser, or a more recent version of a browser you already have, via the Web sites of browser manufacturers. These sites are often good places to look for other Web software too.
Microsoft's home page is at:
**http://www.microsoft.com/**.
Netscape Communications' home page is at:
**http://www.netscape.com/**.

***Netscape Communications' banner***

To download a program, look around the manufacturer's site for a hyperlink which starts the downloading process. For example, if you want a copy of Netscape Navigator, look for a button which is similar to the one below.

 ***Click on this button to download Netscape Navigator.***

To find other software, you can use a search engine (see pages 38 to 41). This is easier if you know the name of the program you are looking for. There is a search engine which searches only for software at:
**http://www.shareware.com/**.

## Downloading preparations

Once you have clicked on a "download" hyperlink, a page will appear asking you to specify what type of computer you have, and what operating system (OS) it is running. (The OS is the group of programs which controls a computer, for example Windows or MacOS.)

You will also be asked which continent and country you live in. If the same program is stored on several different FTP sites, you will have to select a site to download from. Choose a site which is in your part of the world so that the file downloads as quickly as possible.

***There are FTP sites in many different locations.***

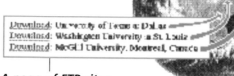

***A page of FTP sites***

You may find your browser can't connect to the FTP site you have chosen. This is because each FTP site has a maximum number of people who can use it at any one time. If this happens, try another site from the list.

## Save As...

Before your computer starts downloading a program, a *Save As...* dialog box will appear on your screen. You must decide where to save the program on your computer's hard disk. If you have a "Programs" directory or folder, save the new software there. If not, you can create a new directory for any software you download. Click *OK* to confirm your choice.

## Downloading

Once you have clicked *OK*, your browser contacts the FTP site, and begins downloading the program. A *Saving Location* window, like the one shown below, will appear on your screen. This gives you information about how the downloading process is progressing.

**This is the URL of the FTP site where the program is stored.**

```
Saving Location                    _ □ ×
Location:   ftp://sunsite.doc...ndows/n32e301.exe
Saving:     C:\TEMP\N32E301.EXE
Status:     1141K of 3547K (at 1.7K/sec)
Time Left:  00:23:59

▮▮▮▮▮▮▮▮▮▮▮▮                        32%

                    [ Cancel ]
```

**This indicates how much of the program has already been downloaded.**

Some programs are very large files, even when they have been compressed (see right). Try to download software when the Internet isn't busy so that it takes less time.

## Compressed programs

Software files are usually compressed or "zipped". This means they have been reduced in size so they take up less space on an FTP site's hard disk. Compressed files can also be transferred from computer to computer more quickly than uncompressed files.

Before you copy any compressed program files from the Net onto your computer, you will need to have a program called a decompressor on your computer's hard disk. This program restores files to their original size so that your computer can use them.

A compressed program is like an inflatable boat with no air inside it. It's easier to store it and carry it around, but you can't use it. A decompressor is like the foot pump that you use to inflate the boat before using it.

## How much does the software cost?

You'll have to pay for some of the software you find on the Net before you can download it. It usually costs as much as if you bought the same software in a store.

Some of the software which is available via the Web is free or costs very little.

 **Freeware** This is software which is free for anyone to copy onto their computer and use.

 **Shareware** This is software which you can download for free. By doing this, you automatically accept certain conditions. A common condition is that you will pay for a program if you decide to keep using it after an initial trial period of 30 days.

 **Trialware** You can try out this software for free, but it contains a device which prevents you from using it fully. Some programs have features which don't work. Others contain a built-in timer which stops the whole program from working after an initial trial period. If you decide to keep the program, you pay the company who made it. They will send you a registration number. This is a code which makes the program work properly.

 **Betaware** This is new software, that needs to be tested. It may not work properly. If you find a fault in a Beta program, you should tell the company that created it. Some beta programs are free; others are charged for.

# Plug-ins

People who create Web pages sometimes make them more exciting by including sounds, moving images and animation. To do this, they use pieces of software called "plug-ins".

## What is a plug-in?

A plug-in is a small program which works with a browser to give it an extra ability. For example, you can add a plug-in to your browser to enable it to show video clips.

If a Web page has been created using a particular plug-in, you will need to add that plug-in to your browser in order to see all the information on the page.

## Animation

A plug-in called Shockwave™ enables you to see animations on Web pages. Shockwave also allows you to enjoy simple games and "interactive" features. Interactive means you can change things on the page by clicking with your mouse. For example, in the game shown below, you can "roll" the dice.

You can download Shockwave from:
**http://www.macromedia.com/shockwave/**.

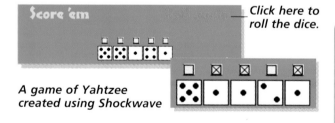

**Click here to roll the dice.**

*A game of Yahtzee created using Shockwave*

## Video

Apple's Quicktime plug-in allows you to watch videos included on Web pages. You can also use it to see some animations and hear some sound effects. You will find Quicktime at:
**http://www.quicktime.apple.com/**.

Videos are very big files. It may take a long time to download even a very short video clip.

## Sound

The RealAudio®plug-in enables your browser to play sound effects and music clips on Web pages. You can also use it to hear Web radio and live concerts that are broadcast over the Web. The Real Audio home page is at:
**http://www.realaudio.com/index.html**.

*Using RealAudio to listen to Web radio*

*The RealAudio player lets you control what you hear.*

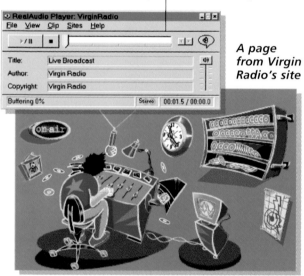

*A page from Virgin Radio's site*

## Streaming

There are two ways in which sound and moving images can be sent from a Web server to your computer.

The first method of sending the information is called streaming. This is like watching TV or listening to the radio. You hear sounds or see images as your computer receives the data.

Alternatively, you may have to download all the data before you can hear or see the information. Once the data is stored on your computer, you can play the sounds or images over and over again, as if you had a CD or a video.

## Downloading and installing

You may see a hyperlink on a site's home page which says something like "Get Shockwave". This means you need that particular plug-in to see all the information on the site. If you don't have the plug-in, you can usually download it by clicking on the hyperlink.

Alternatively, you can obtain a variety of plug-ins which work with your browser via your browser manufacturer's site.

When you download a plug-in, instruct your computer to save it in the "Temp" directory or folder on your computer's hard disk.

Once you have downloaded a plug-in, you will need to install it so that your browser knows it is on your computer. First shut down your browser, then open up the Temp directory, double-click on the plug-in's file name and follow the on-screen instructions.

When your browser was originally installed, it created a special directory or folder called "Plug-ins" on your computer's hard disk. You will find this plug-ins directory in the directory that has the same name as your browser.

During the installation of a new plug-in, your computer usually automatically stores it in the Plug-ins directory. Sometimes you have to tell your computer where this directory is.

## Moving plug-ins

If you don't use a particular plug-in very often, you should move it from the Plug-ins directory to another part of your computer's hard disk. This is because plug-ins use up a lot of RAM (see page 10). If you keep a lot of plug-ins in the Plug-ins directory, your browser will work more slowly than usual. You can move a plug-in back to the Plug-ins directory whenever you want to use it.

## Java™

Some Web pages contain Java "applets". These are tiny programs written in a computer programming language called Java.

Java applets bring Web pages to life. They can contain moving charts and graphs which update themselves, short animations and interactivity.

*An interactive java applet*

**TICKLE ME!**

*Use your mouse to "tickle" Elmo...*

*...then watch him wriggle!*

To run a Java applet you need a browser, such as Microsoft Internet Explorer 4 or Netscape Navigator 4.03, which can understand Java. If your browser doesn't understand Java, you should download one which does from the Web (see pages 44 to 45).

Java is American slang for coffee. It's a suitable name for this programming language because coffee makes people feel energetic, and Java applets make Web pages more lively.

Some Web sites are available in two versions: one with Java applets and one without. The version which doesn't contain Java is sometimes called the "decaffeinated" version, because decaffeinated coffee doesn't make people feel more lively.

# *Personalizing your browser*

You can change the way your browser looks and performs to suit your personal preferences. This is known as customizing your browser.

## *Your default page*

If you find a Web page that you like and decide that you want to see it every time you launch your browser, you can make it your browser's default page (see page 27). Here's how to do this:

 Select *Preferences...* from the *Edit* menu. A dialog box will appear on your screen. Choose *Navigator* from the directory tree on the left so that the *Navigator* form appears on the right.

In the *Home page* section on the *Navigator* form, there is a box called *Location:*. Insert the URL of your chosen default page in this box, then click *OK*.

**Personalizing Netscape Navigator's default page**

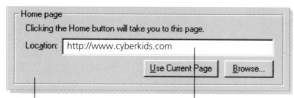

**The Home page section**

**Type the URL of your chosen page here.**

*You will see your chosen page each time you launch your browser.*

  You need to be on-line to change the default page. Download your chosen page so it appears in your browser window. Select *Options* from the *View* menu. A dialog box containing several forms appears on your screen. On the *Navigation* form, there is a section called *Customize*. Select *Start Page* from the drop-down menu, then click on the *Use Current* button. Finally, click *OK*.

## *Your tool bar*

You can choose whether the buttons on your browser's tool bar have words or pictures on them. To do this, follow the instructions below:

 Use the *Appearance* form in the *Preferences...* dialog box. In the *Show toolbar as* section, you can select either P*ictures Only*, *Text Only* or *Pictures and Text*.

 The buttons on the tool bar always have both pictures and words on them. However, you can hide the words by dragging the bottom of the tool bar upwards, as shown below.

**The Microsoft Internet Explorer tool bar**

**Drag the bottom of the tool bar up from here to hide the address box and the words on the tool bar.**

**Drag this label down to see the address box again.**

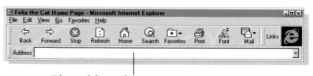

**The address box reappears.**

# Your browser's cache

Your browser stores a copy of every Web page it downloads in the "cache". This is an area of your computer's memory where frequently used data is stored.

## Off-line viewing

You can look at a Web page which is stored in the cache without going on-line. This is called off-line viewing. It's a good idea to get used to viewing Web pages off-line if you have to pay for the time you spend on-line.

While you are on-line, let Web pages download fully, but read them quickly to decide which hyperlinks you want to follow. Once you have disconnected, you can study the pages in the cache for as long as you like.

The pages are stored in a directory or folder called Cache. On a PC, you will find this in the directory that has the same name as your browser. On a Macintosh, it is stored in the Preferences folder (inside the System folder).

To view a page off-line, double-click on its file name in the cache folder. Your browser will start automatically.

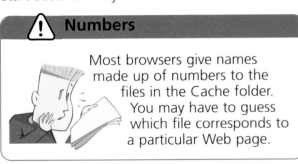

### ⚠ Numbers

Most browsers give names made up of numbers to the files in the Cache folder. You may have to guess which file corresponds to a particular Web page.

## Cache size

Only part of the cache is set aside for your browser. Once its part is full, your browser will delete some of the pages which are stored there in order to make room for new pages. You may want to make your browser's part of the cache bigger so that your browser can store more pages. This will reduce the amount of time you spend on-line, because it takes less time for your browser to fetch a page from the cache than from a Web server.

## Changing the cache size

You can only make your browser's cache bigger if your computer has some free RAM (see page 10). To set aside more RAM for your browser's cache, follow the instructions below. Be careful not to increase the size of the cache too much, as this may slow down your computer.

 Open the *Preferences...* dialog box and find the *Cache* form. (It's under *Advanced* in the directory tree.) The box called *Disk Cache* shows how many bytes have been set aside by your browser for storing downloaded pages. To make the cache bigger, highlight the number in the box and type in a larger number. It is a good idea to increase the number 500 KB at a time.

 Open the *Options* dialog box and click on the tab of the *Advanced* form. Then click on the *Settings* button in the *Temporary Internet files* section. In the window that appears, you can see what percentage of the hard disk space is being used. To make the cache bigger, move the marker as shown below. It is best to adjust the size of the cache 2% at a time.

**Use this dialog box to adjust the size of Microsoft Internet Explorer's cache.**

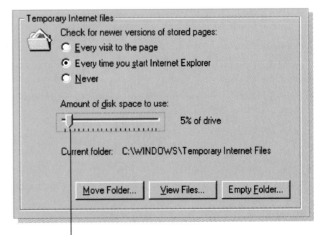

**Move this marker to the right to make the cache bigger.**

# Buying and selling on-line

You can buy a wide variety of things on the Web, such as toys, tickets, clothes, cameras, pizza, and paintings. These pages shows how companies use the Web to find customers.

## Shopping malls

People often buy a lot of different things, such as shoes, gifts, food and books, in one shopping expedition. To do this, it is easier to go to a place called a shopping mall, where you can buy all these things under one roof.

There are shopping malls on the Web too. Each "on-line mall" is a Web site which contains hyperlinks to a wide variety of Web pages where you can buy things. A good example is at:
**http://www.imall.com/**.

Each on-line mall has a "site directory". This is a list of hyperlinks to all the shopping pages in the mall. The hyperlinks are usually categorized according to what the pages sell. Hyperlinks to Web pages that sell footballs, for example, are listed under "sports".

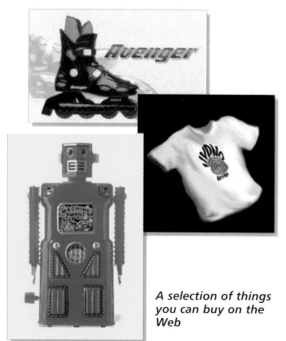

*A selection of things you can buy on the Web*

## Going shopping

Each shopping site contains information about all the things you can buy. You will often see photographs of the products. Some sites even use 3-D pictures so you can look at an object from different angles.

When you find something that you want to buy, you have to order it and pay for it.

*This 3-D dinner service comes from the Virtual Reality Mall (http://www.vr-mall.com/).*

*You can look at it from any angle you choose.*

## Ordering

At some shopping sites, you select any items you want as you browse. You usually do this by placing a mark in a box next to a description of an item. This process is known as carting. At other sites, you make your selection after you have finished looking around the site. To do this, you complete an order form.

*A page from a shopping site*

*A CD*

*This tells you how much the CD costs.*

*Click here to download an order form and to pay.*

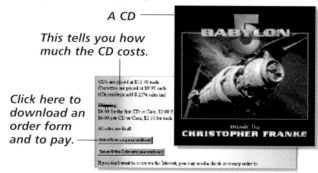

To finish making your order, follow the on-screen instructions. You will have to provide some information, such as your name and address, so that the goods you buy can be delivered to your house.

## Paying

To pay for goods ordered over the Web, you need a bank account. Here are the two most common ways of paying over the Net:

 **Credit cards** This is the most widely used payment method. You enter credit card details onto a payment form on the Web site. This information is then used to remove the money from your bank account.

Before you give out your credit card details, make sure you can see a picture of an  unbroken key somewhere on the Web site. This tells you that the information you supply will be "encrypted" before it is sent across the Net. This means it will be turned into a complicated secret code which only the person to whom you send the information knows how to decode.

 **Digital money** Digital money is made of computer data but it has the same value as ordinary paper and metal money.

Before you go shopping on the Web, you withdraw digital money from your bank account via the Internet and store it on your computer's hard disk. (Ask your bank which software you need to do this.) When you want to buy something through a shopping site, you send the digital money over the Internet to the computer of the person that you have to pay.

### ⚠ Computer crime

 Some people don't think it is safe to send private information over the Internet, even if it is encrypted.

Criminals may be able to intercept an e-mail or a Web page which contains your credit card details. If they worked out how to decode the information, they could use it to steal money from your bank account.

## Entrance fees

Some of the information on the Web is not free for you to use. You have to pay before you can look at it.

For example, to play the games on the Entertainment Online site, you have to "subscribe". This means you pay a monthly fee which allows you to play them as often as you like. However, you can look at other information on the site free of charge.

Entertainment Online is at:
**http://www.e-on.com/**.

*Two of the games you can play at the E-On® site*

*Scottish Open Golf*

*Speedball II*

Other sites use a system called micropayment. You pay a small amount for each piece of information that you use. Some games sites ask you to pay each time you play a game.

## Advertisements

Many Web pages carry advertisements. Advertising is the main reason that most of the information and search services on the Web are free to use.

Companies pay to advertise their products and services on other people's Web pages. This money is usually used to maintain and improve the Web pages where the advertisements are displayed.

# Creating your own Web pages

Why not tell the world about yourself by creating your own pages and putting them on the Web for everyone to see. There are two main ways of doing this. One is with a text editor and a code called HTML (see page 56), the other is with a program called a Web editor.

## A Web editor

A Web editor is a program that helps you build Web pages. The advantage of a Web editor is that it automatically produces the HTML code which turns documents into Web pages. This section shows you how to use two different types of Web editors.

## WYSIWYG Web editors

The most popular type of Web editors are known as WYSIWYG Web editors. WYSIWYG stands for "What you see is what you get". As you build Web pages, a WYSIWYG Web editor shows you what they will look like when viewed through a browser.

With a WYSIWYG Web editor, you start by typing some text into a blank document. You can insert files created in other programs, such as pictures or sounds, whenever you want to.

Once you have a created a basic page, you can reorganize the information on it by dragging pieces of text or pictures into a new position. There are various buttons and menu items that you can use to improve your page's appearance. For example, to change the way a word looks, you can select it with your mouse and click on a button that makes it **bold**.

As you build up a page, a Web editor automatically produces the HTML code that enables a browser to understand and display the information correctly.

*A WYSIWYG editor called Microsoft® FrontPage® Express*

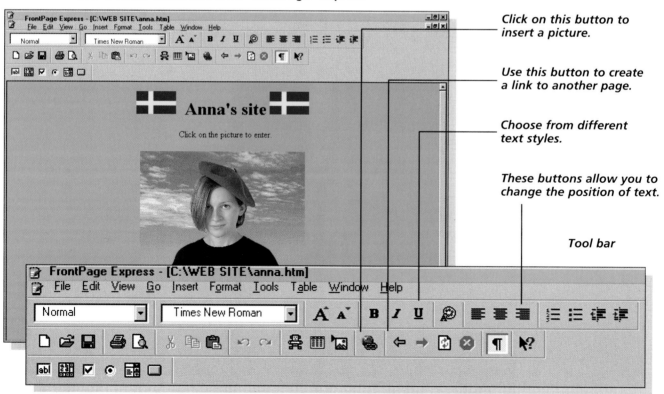

Click on this button to insert a picture.

Use this button to create a link to another page.

Choose from different text styles.

These buttons allow you to change the position of text.

Tool bar

## Building with blocks

Some Web editors, such as Hotdog Express, work differently. Hotdog Express is designed specially for beginners. It uses blocks that represent a part of a Web page, such as a paragraph of text, a picture or a horizontal line.

To build up a Web page, you place the blocks in the order you wish the different parts to appear. You use a dialog box to specify what you want a particular image or piece of text to look like. At any time, you can instruct Hotdog Express to show you what your page will look like on the Web.

*Hotdog Express*

*Use this screen to build up a Web page.*

*Click here to see a preview.*

*This is a preview of the Web page the program has produced.*

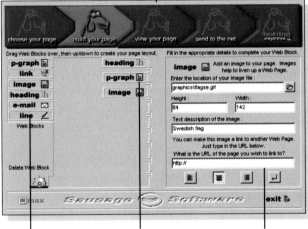

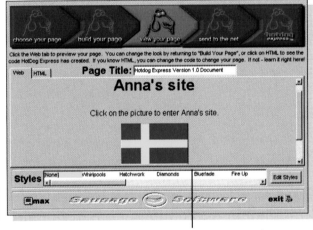

*Choose a block from here.*

*Arrange the blocks here.*

*Use this dialog box to give details about each part of your page.*

*Use this section to select a background for your page.*

---

## Obtaining a Web editor

Here is some information that will help you get hold of a Web editor:

**Where can I find a Web editor?**
On page 97, there is a list of Web sites from which you can order or download Web editors. Alternatively, you can use a "search engine" to find similar sites. This is a program which searches the Web for pages containing a particular word or words, such as **Web editor**. There is a list of search engines on page 96.

**How much will it cost?**
Some Web editors are free of charge. For example, Microsoft FrontPage Express, shown on page 52, comes free with Microsoft's browser, Internet Explorer 4.0.

There are also many Web editors that you have to pay for, but you can try out most of them free of charge for a limited period of time. It is a good idea to test several different programs in this way before you spend any money.

# Planning your Web site

Before you start building a Web site, you should plan it carefully. Decide what kind of information you are going to include, and how you are going to organize it. Before you use your computer, jot down your ideas on paper so that you can figure out the best way of presenting them.

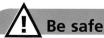 **Be safe**

Millions of Web users will be able to see the information on your Web site. Don't include anything private, such as your home address or telephone number.

## Decide content

With the Web, you aren't restricted to using words to share information with other people. You can use sounds and pictures too. For example, if you are a musician, you could include a short recording of your music. If you belong to a club, you could use photographs to introduce its members, or to show the sort of activities it arranges. You could also add a chart detailing future events.

You can also use photographs or pictures created on a computer to decorate your Web pages. Pictures created on a computer are known as computer graphics.

## Organize content

Decide how many pages your Web site is going to contain and divide up your content between them. Give each page a title which indicates the information it will contain, for example, "About Usborne Publishing" or "Computer Guides". This will help you decide where each piece of information fits best.

## How long?

Don't try to put too much information on one page. There should be enough content to fill at least one screen. But if you have to scroll down more than two screens to reach the bottom of a page, you should divide up the information into a few shorter pages instead.

*Here are some of the things that you can include on your Web site.*

**Sounds – Find out how to insert sounds on page 73.**

**Backgrounds – Discover how to add attractive backgrounds on page 69.**

**Hyperlinks – Page 71 explains how to include picture links.**

**Photographs – Learn how to include photographs on page 68.**

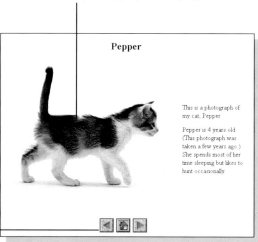

## Design a layout

It is a good idea to design your Web site on paper first. Making sketches like the ones shown above will help you decide where to put pictures in relation to text.

## Include a home page

Once you know what you are going to put on your site, you can plan a "home page". This is an introductory page which tells visitors what information your site contains. It can also include information such as when a site was built or updated.

**A home page**

**This picture links to a page about music.**  **This one links to a page containing photographs.**

**Follow this link to see a page about soccer.**  **Click here to send a message to the creator of the site.**

## Type in your information

Once you have planned your Web site on paper, you need to start putting the information into your computer. The program you will use for this depends on which of the methods for building Web sites you have chosen (see page 52).

If you have decided not to learn HTML, you will need to use a Web editor.

If you have decided to learn HTML, you can type the information in any text editor or word processing program.

Either way, you should always create a separate document for each of your pages.

## Saving a Web page

Even a small Web site can be made up of several files. You may want to create a new directory or folder on your computer's hard disk where you can save each file as you create it. Each file should have a name that is no more than eight letters and numbers long.

If you are using a Web editor, it will automatically save your work as a Web page when you use the *Save* button or menu item.

If you are using a text editor or word processing program, you need to instruct it how to save your work by entering particular information into the Save As dialog box. First make sure *Plain Text* or *Text Documents* is selected in the *Save file as type* field. To specify that the file is a Web page, add the file extension **.htm** to the filename.

**Notepad's Save As dialog box**

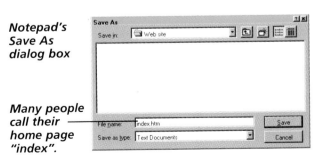

**Many people call their home page "index".**

# HTML

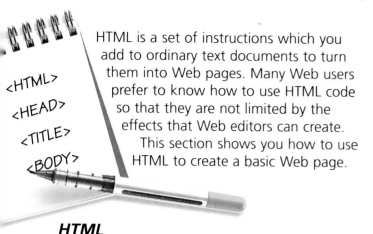

HTML is a set of instructions which you add to ordinary text documents to turn them into Web pages. Many Web users prefer to know how to use HTML code so that they are not limited by the effects that Web editors can create. This section shows you how to use HTML to create a basic Web page.

## HTML

HTML instructions tell a browser that a document is a Web page, and how the information on it should be displayed. For example, there are HTML instructions which tell a browser where to place the text on the page. There are other HTML instructions which dictate how the words should appear.

## Tags

An HTML instruction is called a tag. Tags usually come in pairs – an opening part and a closing part. The opening part comes before the words that are affected by the instruction, and the closing part goes after them. In this example, the tag affects the word "Maria".

Opening part — `<B> Maria </B>` — Closing part

Each part of a tag is put inside these two symbols: < >. They are known as angle brackets. In the example, B instructs a browser to display Maria in bold type. The closing part of a tag always includes a forward slash </ >.

You can type tags in capital letters or small letters. However, it's a good idea to use capital letters so that the tags stand out from the content of a document. This makes it easier to find and alter tags when you want to make changes to your Web pages.

## A Web page source document

Connect your computer to the Internet and download a Web page. Notice that you can't see any HTML tags when you look at a Web page through a browser.

The HTML for a particular Web page is known as its source document. To see the source document of a Web page, select *Page Source* from the *View* menu. Don't be scared by what you see. HTML looks confusing but it's quite easy to use.

*Yahoo!'s home page and its source*

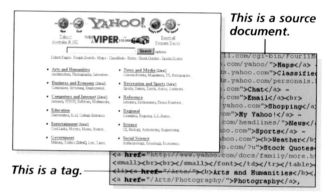

This is a source document.

This is a tag.

## A universal code

HTML is "platform-independent". This means that any type of computer can understand it. It doesn't matter what kind of computer is used to write it. If you have a Mac, you can look at a Web page that was created on an IBM compatible PC.

*An IBM compatible PC and a Mac displaying the same Web page*

PC          Mac

## Essential code

Some essential tags appear in every source document. The tags shown below must appear at the top of a document.

```
<HTML>
<HEAD>
<TITLE>        page title        </TITLE>
</HEAD>
<BODY>
```

In your text editor, open up your home page document. Type the above sequence of tags at the top. Choose a suitable title for your page, for example "Maria's home page", and type it where the words "page title" appear above. Next, type these two tags at the bottom of your document:

```
</BODY>
</HTML>
```

When you have finished, save your document. It should now look similar to the source document shown below.

## Using your browser

You can now look at your document through your browser. To do this, start your browser without connecting to the Internet. Select *Open Page...* from the *File* menu. Click on the *Choose File...* button. Use the dialog box that appears to find your document, then highlight its name and click *Open*. Your document will appear inside your browser window as a Web page, similar to the one in the picture below.

## Other tags

Over the next pages, you will discover some tags that enable you to change the appearance of the words on a Web page, and to add pictures, sounds and hyperlinks.

To add any of these tags to your source document, open it with your text editor. When you have finished making changes, save the file. You can see the changes by opening the file in your browser again, or by clicking on your browser's *Reload* button.

**A source document and the Web page it produces**

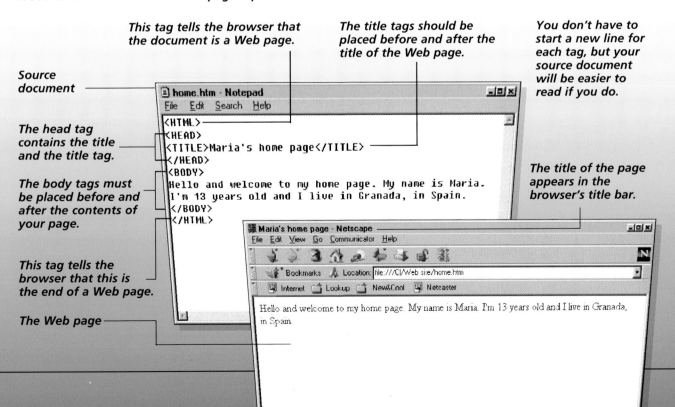

**Source document**

This tag tells the browser that the document is a Web page.

The title tags should be placed before and after the title of the Web page.

You don't have to start a new line for each tag, but your source document will be easier to read if you do.

The head tag contains the title and the title tag.

The body tags must be placed before and after the contents of your page.

This tag tells the browser that this is the end of a Web page.

The Web page

The title of the page appears in the browser's title bar.

# Special effects with text

These pages show you some tags that change the appearance of the text on a Web page.

## Dividing up text

It is difficult to read large amounts of text on a computer screen. To make it easier for Web users to look at your page, you should divide up long pieces of text into smaller sections.

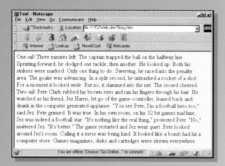

Large areas of text on a Web page look dull and are hard to read.

You can divide up text by instructing a browser to start a new paragraph or a new line. The tags that you use to do this have only one part. They are known as standalones.

To tell a browser to start a new paragraph, type <P> in front of the first word of the paragraph in the source document. Browsers display a blank line between two paragraphs.

To tell a browser to start a new line, type <BR> where you want it to begin.

*A source document and its Web page*

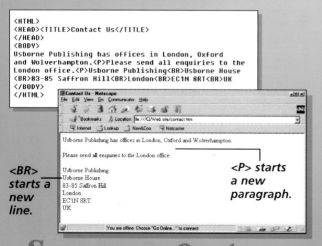

*<BR> starts a new line.*

*<P> starts a new paragraph.*

## White space

It is easier to work with a source document that contains plenty of white space. You can use the Return key as often as you like to create white space in your source documents. This will not affect the appearance of your Web pages. Browsers will only break up the text on Web pages when they are instructed to do so by tags.

*Both these source documents produce the same Web page.*

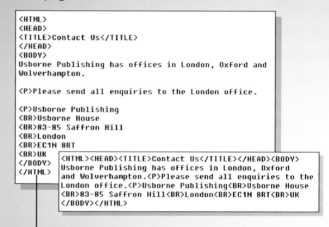

*This source is much easier to read.*

## Emphasizing text

You can use bold and italic type to make important words on your page stand out from the rest of the text.

Your text editor may contain buttons or menu items that convert words into bold or italic type. However, when a browser displays a Web page, it ignores any special effects created using these tools. It will only recognize instructions that are given in HTML.

To instruct a browser to display a piece of text in bold type, type <B> before the text and </B> after it, like this:<B>Usborne</B>.

To instruct a browser to display a piece of text in italic type, type <I> before the text and </I> after it, like this: <I>Usborne</I>.

## Letter size

You can also emphasize a word by altering the size of its letters. There are seven letter sizes, known as font sizes, to choose from. Size 1 is the smallest and size 7 is the biggest.

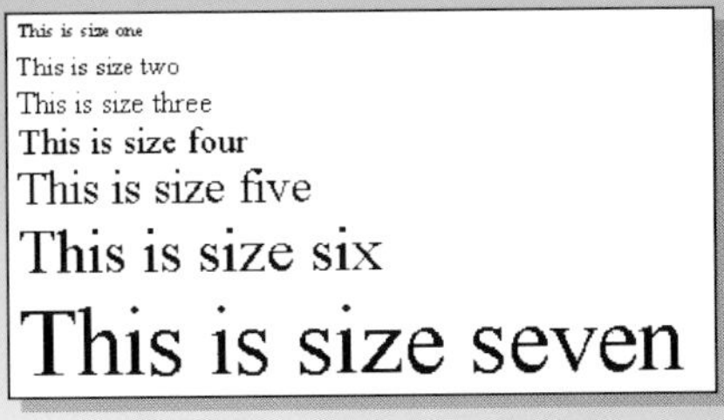

This is size one
This is size two
This is size three
This is size four
This is size five
This is size six
# This is size seven

*This picture compares the seven font sizes.*

To change a section of text into size 6 font, you would type <FONT SIZE="6"> in front of it and </FONT> after it. To use a different font size, simply replace 6 with another number.

## Heading

It is a good idea to use headings to introduce the different sections of text on a Web page. Headings help visitors to your site find information that interests them quickly.

There are six sizes of headings. Level 1 is the biggest and level 6 is the smallest. Levels 1, 2 and 3 are usually used for titles.

*Using headings helps divide up text.*

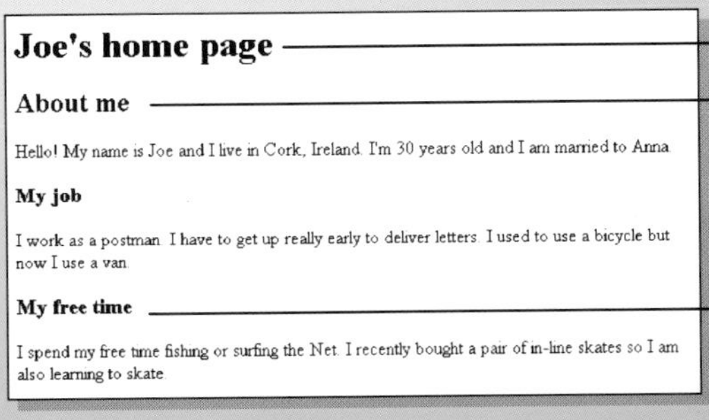

**Joe's home page** ——————————— level 1

**About me** ——————— level 2

Hello! My name is Joe and I live in Cork, Ireland. I'm 30 years old and I am married to Anna

**My job**

I work as a postman. I have to get up really early to deliver letters. I used to use a bicycle but now I use a van.

**My free time** ——————— level 3

I spend my free time fishing or surfing the Net. I recently bought a pair of in-line skates so I am also learning to skate

To turn a piece of text into a level 1 heading, type <H1> in front of the text and </H1> after it. For other heading levels, use the same tag but replace 1 with the appropriate number.

## Which tag?

Although both heading tags and <FONT SIZE> tags change the size of text, they aren't interchangeable.

A heading tag should only be used to change the size of section headings. It belongs to a group of tags known as block level elements. Browsers automatically leave blank lines after block level elements.

A <FONT SIZE> tag should be used for all other text. It belongs to a group of tags known as text level elements. These tags affect only the look of the text, not its position on the page.

You can find lists of other block level and text level elements on Web sites that tell you more about HTML (see page 96).

## Combining tags

When you place more than one tag around a piece of text, it is important to insert the tags in the correct order, as shown below.

*Two tags placed correctly*

**A tag can contain another tag.**

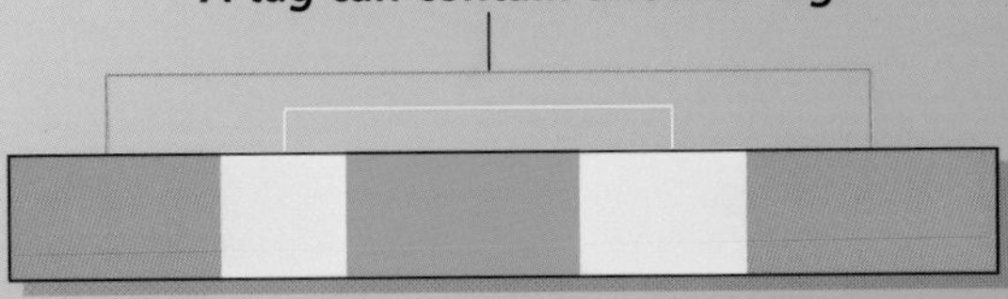

*Two tags placed incorrectly*

**Tags must not overlap each other.**

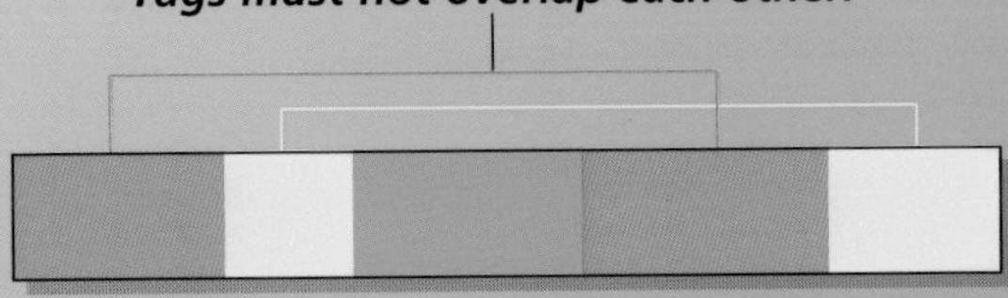

Block level elements can contain other block level elements or text level elements. Text level elements can only contain other text level elements.

# Color

Unless instructed otherwise, a browser will display text in black on a gray or white background. To make your Web site look more attractive, you can specify different colors for the background and the text.

## Describing colors

When people describe colors, they use adjectives such as light, dark and bright to distinguish between different shades. A computer, on the other hand, describes colors using combinations of letters and numbers known as hexadecimal color codes. These codes are always made up of 6 characters. For example, the code 000000 describes black.

A tag that instructs a browser to use a particular color must always contain a hexadecimal color code.

## Color codes

You can find addresses of Web sites that list hexadecimal codes on page 97, but here are a few to get you started:

## How many colors?

It is estimated that hexadecimal codes can describe around 16 million different colors but most computers can't show this many.

The number of colors a computer monitor can show depends on the type of video card inside the processing unit. Most Web users have computers that contain 8-bit or 16-bit video cards. An 8-bit card can display 256 colors and a 16-bit card can display 65,536.

If a computer can't display the exact shade specified in a source document, it will show the nearest color that it can display.

## Background

To change the background color of a Web page, you need to insert some extra code into the opening part of its <BODY> tag.

Imagine you want the background of a page to be the shade of blue which is described by the code 87CEEB. If you replace <BODY> with <BODY BGCOLOR="#87CEEB">, your browser will display the page with a blue background.

*This picture shows a source and the Web page with a colored background that it produces.*

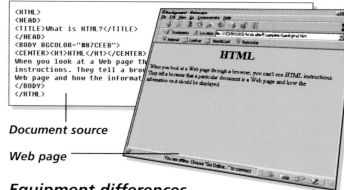

Document source

Web page

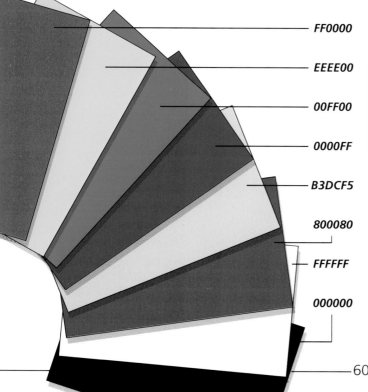

FF0000

EEEE00

00FF00

0000FF

B3DCF5

800080

FFFFFF

000000

## Equipment differences

Colors appear brighter on a Mac computer than on an IBM compatible PC. A Web page designed on a Mac will appear slightly duller on a PC.

## Text color

You can change the color of all the text on a page by adding some code to the <BODY> tag. For example, to instruct a browser to display the text on a page in red, add TEXT= "#FF0000" to the opening part of the body tag, as follows: <BODY TEXT= "#FF0000">. The closing part of the tag remains unchanged.

## Highlight a section of text

You can instruct a browser to display a section of text, a word or a single letter in a particular color. For example, to turn a piece of text blue, type <FONT COLOR="#0000FF"> in front of the text that you want to change. Then type </FONT> after this text to close the tag. The rest of the text on the page won't be affected.

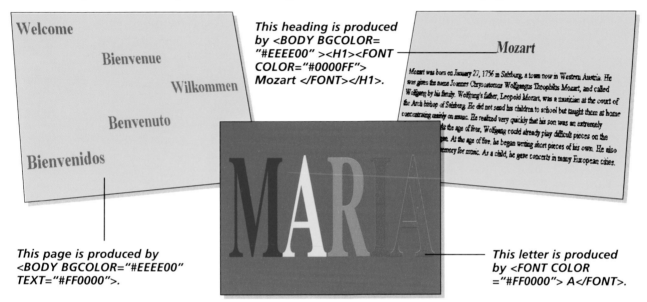

*This heading is produced by <BODY BGCOLOR= "#EEEE00" ><H1><FONT COLOR="#0000FF"> Mozart </FONT></H1>.*

*This page is produced by <BODY BGCOLOR="#EEEE00" TEXT="#FF0000">.*

*This letter is produced by <FONT COLOR ="#FF0000"> A</FONT>.*

## Color advice

It is fun to experiment with different text and background colors. However, before you settle for a particular combination, make sure that all the text on your page is easy to read. Dark colors, such as navy blue or black, look good on a white or pastel background. Light colors, such as white or yellow, show up clearly on a dark background.

Avoid large amounts of very bright colors such as red (FF0000) or shocking pink (FF69B4). People may not bother to explore your site thoroughly if you make it difficult for them to read the information it contains.

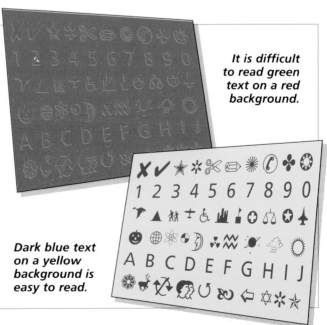

*It is difficult to read green text on a red background.*

*Dark blue text on a yellow background is easy to read.*

# *Organizing information*

You can use a variety of devices, such as lists or lines, to organize the text on a Web page.

## Lists

There are three types of lists that you can include on a Web site: ordered lists, unordered lists and definition lists.

## Ordered lists

You should create an ordered list when the items in your list need to appear in a particular order, for instance, classes on a timetable.

Type <OL> before the text which you want to turn into an ordered list and </OL> after it. Then type <LI> in front of each item in the list. Browsers will display a number in front of each item, as shown in the picture below.

The code for the list shown below is: <OL> <LI>English<LI>Biology<LI>Physics<LI>German <LI>Art<LI>History<LI>Geography</OL>.

If you add another item anywhere in an ordered list, browsers will automatically renumber all the items appropriately.

*An ordered list*

1. English
2. Biology
3. Physics
4. German
5. Art
6. History
7. Geography

## Unordered lists

Use an unordered list for items of equal importance, such as items in a shopping list.

To create an unordered list, type <UL> before the text and </UL> after it. Then type <LI> in front of each item in the list. For example, <UL><LI>strawberry<LI>blackberry<LI>lemon <LI>apple<LI>plum</UL>. Browsers will display a dot known as a bullet point in front of each item.

*An unordered list*

- strawberry
- blackberry
- lemon
- apple
- plum

## Definition lists

A definition list is ideal for a collection of words and their meanings, such as a glossary.

To create a definition list, type <DL> before all the text and </DL> after it. Then type <DT> in front of each term that is defined and <DD> in front of each definition. Browsers display each definition on a new line.

The code for the definition list shown here is: <DL><DT>Winter<DD>The coldest season of the year<DT>Summer<DD>The warmest season of the year</DL>.

*A definition list*

Winter
    The coldest season of the year
Summer
    The warmest season of the year

## Quotations

A block quote tag tells browsers to separate a particular section of text from the other text on a Web page. It is often used to indicate quotations which are words written or said by somebody else.

**A block quote tag places text in the middle of a page.**

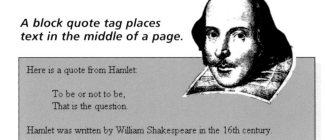

Here is a quote from Hamlet:

> To be or not to be,
> That is the question.

Hamlet was written by William Shakespeare in the 16th century.

To turn a piece of text into a block quote, type <BLOCKQUOTE> before it and </BLOCKQUOTE> after it.

## Arranging text

Browsers can line text up with the left or right side of a page. This is known as aligning text.

**Aligned text**

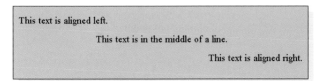

This text is aligned left.

This text is in the middle of a line.

This text is aligned right.

To align a piece of text, you need to insert an extra instruction in the <P> or heading tag that appears before it (see pages 58 to 59).
For example, if you want to align text left, type <P ALIGN="LEFT">. To align text right, type RIGHT instead of LEFT.

Browsers can also place text in the middle of a line. To instruct a browser to do this, type <CENTER> in front of the text and </CENTER> after the text. For example <CENTER>This text is in the middle of a line </CENTER>.

## Horizontal lines

Horizontal lines or "rules" can be used to divide up your page into sections. To insert a horizontal rule, you use a standalone tag: <HR>. Type this tag wherever you want a rule to appear. Browsers automatically display a thin rule that extends all the way across a Web page.

You can change a rule's appearance by adding extra information to its <HR> tag. For example, to instruct a browser to display a rule that is half as wide as a page, type <HR WIDTH="50%">. (You can change the percentage as required.)

To change a rule's thickness, type: <HR SIZE =?>, replacing ? with a number. The higher the number, the thicker the rule.

Browsers automatically place rules in the middle of a line. To alter a rule's position, add ALIGN="LEFT" or ALIGN="RIGHT" to its <HR> tag. Try out different instructions to find a rule that looks good on your page.

**A variety of horizontal rules**

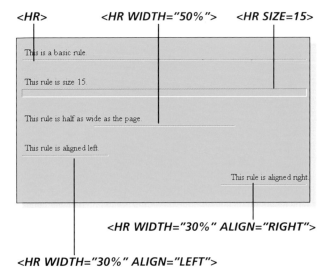

**<HR>**   **<HR WIDTH="50%">**   **<HR SIZE=15>**

This is a basic rule.

This rule is size 15.

This rule is half as wide as the page.

This rule is aligned left.

This rule is aligned right.

**<HR WIDTH="30%" ALIGN="RIGHT">**

**<HR WIDTH="30%" ALIGN="LEFT">**

# Pictures on the Web

One of the reasons the Web is such a popular source of information is because it contains pictures. Here are some of the ways in which pictures can be used on a Web site.

## A picture gallery

Some Web sites contain a gallery section where pictures are displayed. This may include a page of "thumbnails", which are small versions of the images that are displayed elsewhere on the site. If you decide you want to see a larger version of a picture, you can click on its thumbnail to download it.

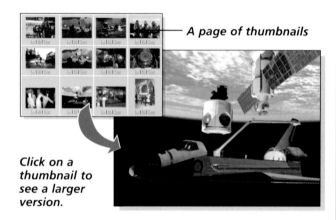

— *A page of thumbnails*

*Click on a thumbnail to see a larger version.*

## Decorative dividers

Long, thin pictures, known as bars, can be used to divide up different sections of information on a Web page.

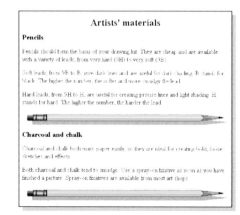

*A bar has the same function as a rule but looks more interesting.*

## Backgrounds

You can use computer graphics to create attractive backgrounds. A background is usually made from a small graphic, called a tile, that a browser displays over and over again.

Patterns that don't distract your visitor's attention from the text, and that fit in well with the theme of the page, look best.

*This page has a background that looks like water.*

*This tile is repeated to create the background.*

## Indicate links

A picture can be a hyperlink to another Web page. For example, a picture of a house, such as the ones shown here, is often used as a hyperlink to a site's home page. A small picture that represents the page to which it connects is known as an icon.

*A selection of home page icons*

## Obtaining pictures

There are many pictures on the Web that you can copy and include on your site. You can find collections of backgrounds, bars, buttons and icons. To do this, use a search engine to carry out a key word search.

Alternatively, you can visit one of the sites listed on page 96. You will find instructions for copying pictures off the Web onto your computer on page 35.

*You will find these icons at*
*http://aplusart.simplenet.com/aplusart/index.html*

## Copyright

Not all of the pictures on the Web are free for you to use. Much of the information on the Web is "copyrighted". This means a particular person or organization controls the ways in which copies of the information are used.

If you want to put copyrighted information on your Web site, you must first contact the organization that owns the copyright and obtain their permission. If you don't do this, you may be breaking the law.

*This sign usually appears on a Web site when the information is copyrighted.*

## Free information

Some information, known as public domain information, is not copyrighted.

The pictures in the collections listed on page 97 are in the public domain. If you find any other picture collections, make sure the pictures are available for public use before including any of them in your site.

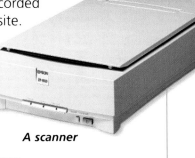

*A selection of copyright free images from http://www.nasa.gov/*

## Digital pictures

You may want to include your own drawings or photographs on your site. Before you do this, you have to record them in digital code. This is a number code that computers can understand. You can only put pictures that are recorded digitally on a Web site.

Pictures can be converted into digital code by a machine called a scanner. This process is called scanning in. You can find out more about it on page 66.

*A scanner*

Scanners are quite expensive, but you don't have to buy one. You can have your pictures scanned at most photocopying shops or photograph processing business. Alternatively, you can hire a scanner from a computer hardware store and scan in your pictures yourself.

# Preparing pictures

When you scan in a picture, you create an image file that you can insert into a Web page. This section explains how to create image files and adapt them for use on the Web.

## How does a scanner work?

A scanner is attached to a computer. Software on the computer tells the scanner how to collect and save information about a picture. This software is known as image-editing or imaging software.

The scanner divides a picture into tiny dots known as picture elements or pixels. It gathers information about the color and position of each one. It then records this information in digital code so that the computer can reproduce the picture. You use imaging software to tell a scanner how many pixels to divide a picture into. The number of pixels in an image is known as its resolution. It is usually measured in dots per inch (dpi).

*Pixels*

*When you look at a digital image close up, the pixels are clearly visible.*

Imaging software also lets you alter or "edit" digital images, and create images from scratch. You can find out how to obtain an image-editing program on page 97.

## File size

When creating picture files for use on the Web, it is important to make them as small as possible so that they download quickly. The size of a file is measured in bytes.

## Resolution

You can control the size of an image file by changing its resolution. A "high" resolution image contains a lot of pixels so it produces a large file. A "low" resolution image contains fewer pixels so it is contained in a smaller file.

You can see the difference between a high resolution and low resolution image when you print them out.

*Compare the quality of a high resolution picture to the quality of a low resolution picture.*

*This is a high resolution image. It was scanned in at 350 dpi.*

*This is a low resolution image. It was scanned in at 72 dpi.*

High resolution and low resolution images look very similar on a computer monitor. When you prepare a picture for use on the Web, scan it in at 72 or 75 dpi. Low resolution images are good enough for use on the Web.

## Saving pictures

Imaging software can save pictures in many different ways. The most popular types of picture files used on the Web are Graphical Interchange Format (GIF) and Joint Photographic Experts Group (JPEG) format.

*This picture of the Chicago Museum of Science and Industry (http://www.msichicago.org/) is a JPEG file.*

## GIF

GIF files are usually used for pictures that have large proportions of one color, or that are irregularly shaped. For example, most icons, buttons and bars are GIF files.

*These icons from the Chicago Museum of Science and Industry's site are GIF files.*

GIF files contain a maximum of 256 colors. This helps to make the files small. If a picture contains more than 256 colors, an imaging program reduces the number of colors to save it as a GIF. When you save a picture as a GIF, add the extension **.gif** to the file name.

## JPEG format

JPEG files are ideal for pictures that contain many different colors, such as photographs. They record the information in a way that takes up less space. This is called compression.

JPEG files can be compressed by different amounts. The greater the amount of compression, the smaller the size of the file. However, the amount of compression also affects how good a picture looks. The smaller the amount of compression, the better the quality of the picture.

Try compressing a file by different amounts until you find the smallest file that still looks good. To do this, first save a few different versions of an image by altering the amount of compression each time. When you save a JPEG file, add the extension **.jpg** to the file name.

*A dialog box from an imaging program called Adobe® Photoshop®*

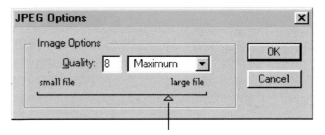

*Move this slider to the left to compress the file.*

Next, open up all the versions at the same time in your imaging program so that you can compare what they look like. Try to keep all your picture files under 30 kilobytes (KB).

## Measurements

When you have inserted a picture into a Web page (see page 68), look at it through your browser. You should be able to see all of it without using the scroll bars.

If necessary, use your imaging program to make a picture smaller. The size of a digital image is measured in pixels. For example, a 40 x 42 icon is 40 pixels across and 42 pixels high. When you resize a picture, make sure you change its height and width in proportion or it will become distorted.

# *Putting pictures on Web pages*

Adding an object, such as a picture or a sound, to a Web page is known as embedding. This section tells you how to embed pictures.

## *Embedding a picture*

Imagine, for example, you want to embed a picture called "martin.jpg" in a Web page. First place the picture file in the same directory as the page's source document on your computer's hard disk. Open up the source document and type <IMG SRC="martin.jpg"> where you want the picture to appear.

You can insert this embedding tag anywhere on a Web page, as long as it is between the two parts of the <BODY> tag.

*A Web page containing a picture and its source*

## *No pictures*

Some people surf the Web with browsers that can't display images. Others instruct their browsers not to display images so they can download pages more quickly.

It is polite to let these people know what the pictures they can't see are like. To do this, you can instruct a browser to display words, known as alternative text, instead of a picture.

*Part of Yahoo!'s home page viewed without images*

**This is alternative text.**

## *Alternative text*

To provide alternative text for a picture, add ALT="alternative text" to its embedding tag. For example, the embedding tag for a picture of an oak tree might look like this <IMG SRC="oak.gif" ALT="oak tree">.

## *Downloading pictures*

When you download a page from the Web, the words on the page usually appear on your screen before the pictures. This is because pictures take longer to travel across the Net.

If a browser knows how wide and how high a picture is going to be, it can leave the right amount of space as it displays the text. Otherwise, it may have to rearrange the text on the page when the picture arrives. You can warn a browser how big a picture is by adding extra information to the embedding tag.

*This picture is still being downloaded.*

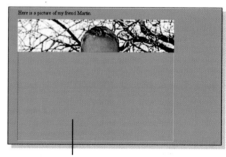

**The browser has drawn a box in which the rest of the picture will appear.**

To do this, first use your image-editing program to find out the picture's dimensions in pixels. Then you can add this information to the picture's embedding tag.

Imagine, for example, you are using a picture which is 180 pixels across and 140 pixels high. Insert WIDTH=180 HEIGHT=140 into the embedding tag. The embedding tag should now look something like this: <IMG WIDTH=180 HEIGHT=140 SRC="martin.jpg">.

## Arranging pictures

To instruct a browser to align a picture left or right, add ALIGN="LEFT" or ALIGN="RIGHT" to the embedding tag. For example, if you wanted to align a picture right, the tag would be similar to this: <IMG WIDTH=180 HEIGHT =180 SRC="bridge.jpg" ALIGN="RIGHT">.

**The picture on this page is aligned.**

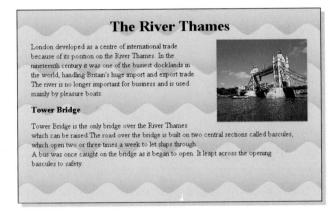

**Notice how the picture pushes the text to the left.**

You can use the <CENTER> tag (see page 63) to instruct a browser to place a picture in the middle of a page. To do this, place the two parts of the tag around the embedding tag. For example, <CENTER><IMG WIDTH=180 HEIGHT=180 SRC="bridge.jpg"></CENTER>.

**When a picture appears in the middle of a Web page, it pushes the text downward.**

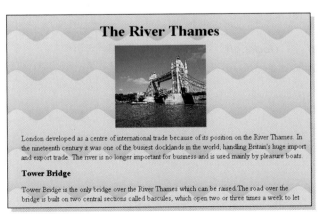

## Reusing pictures

It is a good idea to reuse pictures wherever possible. This brightens up a site without increasing the time it takes to download.

When a browser downloads a Web page, it copies each piece of information onto your computer. So, when a picture appears for a second time, the browser displays the copy that is stored on your computer. It doesn't have to get the information from the Web again.

**Several of the pictures on this site are repeated.**

## Background

To add a patterned background to a page, you need to add some code to the <BODY> tag.

Imagine you want to use a tile called "tile.gif" to form a background for your page. Insert BACKGROUND="tile.gif" in the <BODY> tag, like this: <BODY BGCOLOR ="#FFF8E0" BACKGROUND="tile.gif">.

When you use a patterned background you should also specify a background color for the page. People whose browsers don't show pictures will see this color instead.

# Linking Web pages

Once you have created a few Web pages, you can join them together with hyperlinks. You can also link your pages to other people's sites.

You can make words or pictures into hyperlinks. For example, you could make a hyperlink to the White House Web site from the sentence "Last year, my family and I visited the White House" or from a photograph of the White House.

## Links within a site

Links within a Web site are called local links. They help visitors to find their way around the pages on the site. Each of your pages should contain a link to your home page as well as a selection of links to other pages on your site.

## Links to other sites

Links to other sites are known as remote links. You can use remote links to connect your page to other pages on the same subject or to direct your visitors to sites you have enjoyed.

## Linking tag

You can turn any word, phrase or picture into a hyperlink by using an "anchor tag".

### An anchor tag

`<A HREF="http:www.usborne.co.uk">`

`</A>` ──── *Closing part*        *Opening part*

An anchor tag's opening part tells a browser to download another page and specifies the location of that page. The tag shown above contains a URL. This is because the page to which the link connects belongs to another site.

When you create a local link, the opening part of an anchor tag contains different information. If a page is stored in the same directory, you need only insert its name. For example, <A HREF="music.htm">. If a page is stored in a subdirectory, include the filename and its location. For example, <A HREF="hobbies/music.htm">.

*This picture shows how you can use hyperlinks to jump from one Web site to another.*

**These links are part of the text.**

**A list of interesting and useful sites is called an index.**

## Picture links

To create a picture link, place the two parts of the anchor tag around the tag used to embed the picture (see page 68).

Imagine, for example, you want to transform a picture called "balloon.gif" into a link to this page: **http://www.ballooning.co.uk/**. You would type:
<A HREF="http://www.ballooning.co.uk/">
<IMG SRC="balloon.gif"></A>.

Your browser will display the picture with a border. This indicates that it is a link. Remember that some people's browsers are not set up to show pictures (see page 22). Whenever you use a picture as a hyperlink, always provide a text link as well.

**Click on the balloon to see a page about ballooning.**

**Border**

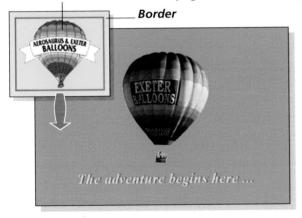

## Remove a border

If you don't like the border that surrounds a picture link, you can instruct a browser not to display it. To do this, add BORDER=0 to the embedding tag. For example, <IMG BORDER=0 SRC="balloon.gif">.

Visitors to your site will still be able to tell that a picture without a border is a hyperlink. When they pass their mouse over it, the pointer will change to a hand symbol, like the one shown here.

## Text links

To create a text link, place the two parts of the anchor tag around the word or phrase that you want to act as a link. For example, to turn the words "White House" into a link to the White House site at **http://www.whitehouse.gov/**, you would type:<A HREF="http://www.white house.gov/">White House</A>.

Your browser will underline the words White House and display them in a different color. This makes it clear they form a hyperlink.

**Click on the underlined text to go to the White House home page.**

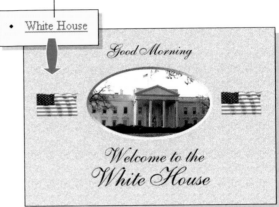

## On the Web

The addresses of Web pages can change, and some pages are removed from the Web altogether. As a result, hyperlinks can become out-of-date or "invalid".

When you click on an invalid hyperlink, an error message will appear on your screen to explain that your browser can't find a page at the address indicated in the anchor tag.

Once your site is on the Web, you should regularly check your links to other people's pages. Be sure to update or remove any invalid hyperlinks so that visitors to your site aren't disappointed or frustrated by them.

# Including sounds

You can record sounds onto your computer and add them to your Web site. To do this, you may need some extra hardware and software.

## Sound hardware

A computer uses a device called a sound card to capture sounds in digital format and play them back. All Macs and multimedia PCs contain sound cards. If you have another kind of computer, you may need to add one. You'll also need headphones or speakers to hear sounds coming from your computer.

*Sound card*

*Speakers*

*Microphone*

To record your own sounds, such as your voice, you will need a microphone that can be plugged into your computer. If you want to record something from a cassette or a CD, you will need a cable to connect your stereo set to your computer.

## Ready-made sounds

You may prefer to use ready-made sound clips on your site. You can find collections of sound clips on CD-ROM and on the Web.
    Before you add a sound clip to your Web site, make sure it is copyright-free (see page 65), or that you have permission from the person who created the sound.

## Sound software

To create your own sound clips, you need a program that allows you to record and edit sound. You may already have such a program on your computer. The example shown below is Sound Recorder, a sound editing program that comes with Windows® 95. If you don't already have a suitable program, or you want a more advanced one, you can download one from the Net (see page 97).

*The Sound Recorder window*

*Click here to start recording a sound.*

*Click here to stop recording.*

## Sound file formats

There are several different types of sound files. The ones that are usually used on the Web are: AU, MIDI, WAV and AIFF.

 AU files work on all types of computers, but they sometimes sound a bit crackly.

 MIDI files work on all types of computers and sound better than AU files.

 WAV is the Microsoft® Windows® audio format. Most browsers can handle these files.

 AIFF is the Macintosh audio file format. Most browsers can play these files.

## Create a sound clip

Use your sound editing program to record and save a sound in a suitable format. Your program may allow you to choose a recording quality. The higher the quality of the recording, the bigger the sound file will be.

Some sound programs enable you to add special effects or mix sounds together. For example, with Sound Recorder, you can add echoes to your sound or reverse it so that you hear everything backward.

**A dialog box from Sound Recorder**

**Choose between CD, Radio or Telephone Quality.**

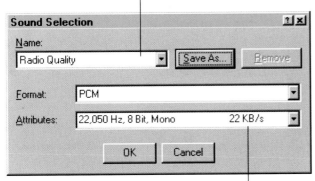

**This tells you how many kilobytes (KB) of disk space one second of the selected sound quality requires.**

## Sound clips on the Web

 Sound files are usually very big files. A few seconds of speech can take up over 100 KB of disk space, even when it is recorded at low quality.

Not all Web users want to spend time downloading sound clips, so it is better to create a hyperlink to a sound file rather than embed it directly in a Web page. Near the hyperlink, you should indicate how big the sound file is, how long it will play for, and what information it contains. This enables visitors to your site to decide whether or not they want to hear the sound clip. If they do, they can click on the hyperlink to download it.

## Link to a sound file

You use an anchor tag to link to a sound file. For example, to turn "Listen to me play the drums (150 KB)" into a link to "drum.wav", you would type: <A HREF="drum.wav"> Listen to me play the drums (150 KB)</A>.

When you follow a link to a sound file, a window containing a device called an audio player appears on screen. This plays sound files. Some audio players start automatically. With others, you have to click on a play button.

**An audio player**

**The slider bar moves across as the sound plays.**

## Embed a sound file

The tag used to insert a sound file into a Web page is: <EMBED SRC="?">. Imagine, for example, you want to embed a sound file called "welcome.wav". To do this you would type: <EMBED SRC="welcome.wav">.

Some browsers will display an audio player in response to this tag. Others will display an icon that you can click on to hear the sound.

**Netscape Navigator displays an icon.**

**The icon**

**Double-click on the icon to hear the sound.**

# Moving images

You can make your Web site more eye-catching by adding moving pictures, such as animations.

## Animation

An animation is a moving image made from a sequence of pictures, known as frames. Each frame is slightly different from the previous one. When they are displayed in quick succession, the objects in the pictures appear to move.

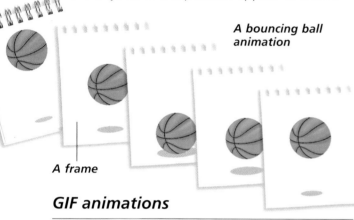

*A bouncing ball animation*

*A frame*

## GIF animations

A GIF animation is produced from a series of GIF files. GIF animations are very popular on the Web. They are easy to create and any browser that can show GIF files can play GIF animations.

## Obtaining GIF animations

On the Web, there are collections of GIF animations that you can use on your Web site for free. To find a GIF animation, perform a search for **animated GIF** or **GIF animation**.

You download and embed GIF animations in the same way as you download and embed ordinary pictures (see pages 35 and 68).

*This animation was saved from http://www.webpromotion.com/.*

## Create your own GIF animations

To create your own GIF animations, you need an imaging program (see page 66) and a "GIF animation editor". This is a program that allows you to build up a sequence of GIF files. (Find out where to obtain one on page 97.)

First plan out your animation on paper. Try to use as few frames as possible to form your animation in order to keep the file size down. It is best not to use more than 12 frames.

Next, create the frames using your imaging program. Save each picture separately in GIF format. When saving animation frames, give each file a name that indicates where it comes in the sequence. This will be helpful when you build up your animation.

*If these frames are shown in this order, the clock's hand goes around clockwise.*

*clock1.gif*        *clock2.gif*        *clock3.gif*        *clock4.gif*

*If they are shown in reverse order, the clock's hand goes around counter-clockwise.*

## Build up a GIF animation

Once you have created all the frames for your animation, use your GIF animation editor to bring them together into a single file.

Animation editors let you control the order in which the frames appear, and how many times over the animation will play. Some programs let you specify other information, such as for how long each frame should appear.

## Java™ applets

Another way to add animation and sound to a Web page is by embedding a Java™ applet (see page 47).

Java applets can contain animation, sound and interactive features. This means you can change things on a Web page by clicking with your mouse. On page 97 there is a list of Web sites where you can find ready-made applets to add to your site.

## Including Java

Web sites that offer free Java applets usually include instructions for embedding them in a Web page.

To see a Java applet in operation, it is best to use Netscape Navigator® 4.03, Microsoft® Internet Explorer 4, or a later version of either of these browsers.

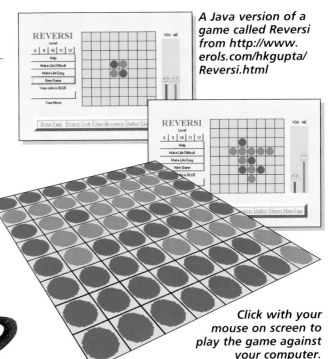

*A Java version of a game called Reversi from http://www. erols.com/hkgupta/ Reversi.html*

*Click with your mouse on screen to play the game against your computer.*

*In this Java applet, the moons whizz around the planet.*

---

### Video

You can embed a video clip into a Web page in the same way as you add a sound clip. However, video clips are more complicated to create and they produce huge files that you or visitors to your site may have trouble downloading.

As home, school and office computers become more and more powerful, video clips will become more popular with Web site builders and users alike.

# Describing your pages

Most people use programs called search engines to find information on the Web. A search engine looks for pages containing specific words and displays a list of the pages it finds. You can add tags to your page that tell a search engine what information your page contains. These tags are known as meta tags.

## Meta tags

The most commonly used meta tags are description meta tags and key words meta tags. A description tag summarizes a page's contents, and a key words tag contains a selection of words that are essential to the content of the page.

Meta tags should be placed between the two parts of the <HEAD> tag at the beginning of a source document. The information inside meta tags will not appear on a Web page.

## Description tag

A description tag for a page about dinosaurs might look like this:

```
< META NAME="description" CONTENT="This site
contains information for children about dinosaurs,
natural history museums with dinosaur exhibits,
dinosaur societies, fossils and palaeontology." >
```

To adapt this tag for your own Web pages, change the words between the second pair of quotation marks. Try to think up a short, clear description that is no more than 20 words long.

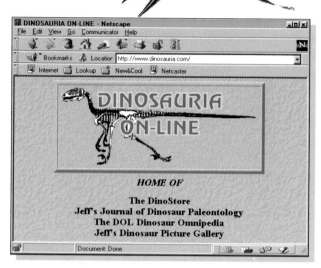

*A Web site about dinosaurs at http://www. dinosauria.com/*

*Some of the key words for this site are "dinosaur", "DinoStore" and "Battatt Museum of Science".*

## Key words tag

Here is a key words tag for an imaginary page about dinosaurs:

```
<META NAME="keywords" CONTENT="dinosaurs,
dinosaur, palaeontology, jurassic, natural history" >
```

You can adapt this tag for your own Web pages by replacing the words between the second pair of quotation marks.

## How does a search engine work?

When a search engine collects information about a new Web page, it looks for meta tags. If it doesn't find any, it will use its own methods to decide what the page is about. For example, it might display the first few words on a Web page as a description of the page's contents.

# Ready for the Web?

Here are some of the things you should do before you put your site on the Web.

## Accuracy and efficiency

You should check your site by carefully rereading each page through your browser.

Ensure that all the information on your site is correct and that there are enough local links to enable visitors to find their way around easily (see page 70).

It isn't easy for you to see your site from a visitor's point of view. Things that appear obvious to you, such as where to find a particular piece of information, may not be obvious to others. If possible, ask a friend to explore your site for you. They may be able to suggest some improvements.

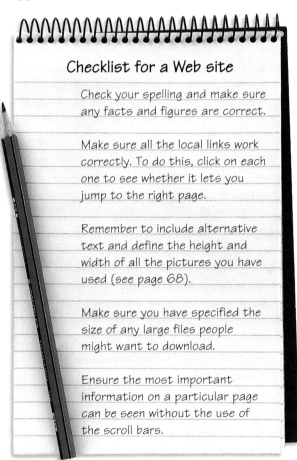

### Checklist for a Web site

Check your spelling and make sure any facts and figures are correct.

Make sure all the local links work correctly. To do this, click on each one to see whether it lets you jump to the right page.

Remember to include alternative text and define the height and width of all the pictures you have used (see page 68).

Make sure you have specified the size of any large files people might want to download.

Ensure the most important information on a particular page can be seen without the use of the scroll bars.

## Filing system

You should store all the files for your Web site in one directory on your computer's hard disk.

If there are a lot of files, you may want to create some subdirectories within your site's main directory. For instance, you could create a subdirectory to hold all the picture files. If you move a file, remember to update the relevant links on your Web pages so that browsers can still locate it. If a browser can't locate a picture file, it displays an icon instead.

*This picture shows the icon Netscape Navigator displays when it can't find a picture file.*

## Use different equipment

A Web page may appear slightly different when it is looked at using a different computer, browser, operating system or type of Net connection. If possible, try out your Web site on a variety of different machines to check that it looks acceptable on all of them.

## Finishing touches

It is important to include the date you finished your site so that visitors know how up-to-date the information it contains is.

Finally, make extra copies of all the files and store them in a safe place. That way, if anything happens to the computer to which you transfer your site, you won't have lost all your hard work.

# Providing Web space

Web sites are stored on powerful computers called servers or hosts. Before people can visit your site, you will have to transfer it to a Web server. Unless you have your own server, you will need to rent space on someone else's.

*A server*

A company that rents out space on Web servers is known as a hosting company. There are two main types of hosting companies: Internet access providers and Web presence providers.

## Internet access providers

Internet access providers (IAPs) are companies that provide access to the Net, such as Internet service providers (ISPs) and on-line services. An ISP only provides access to the Net, whereas an on-line service also provides access to a private network of information.

Most IAPs provide customers with between 1 and 5 megabytes (MB) of space on a Web server. 1MB is just over a million bytes and is enough to store a small personal Web site.

## Web presence providers

Web presence providers are companies that specialize in storing or "hosting" Web sites. They offer large amounts of space and extra services, such as security for sites used to sell things. For this reason, many of their customers are businesses and big organizations.

*These Web presence providers host business Web sites.*

## Making choices

You can find the addresses of Internet access providers and Web presence providers in Internet magazines or on the Web (see page 96). Each company offers a slightly different service and charges different fees.

Here are some questions that you might like to ask before you choose a company to host your Web site:

### How fast will my site download?

Find out how powerful the servers are, and how they are linked to the Net. The more powerful the server, and the greater the bandwidth of the link (see right), the quicker your pages will download.

It's a good idea to visit a hosting company's Web site to see how quickly their own pages download. If they can't deliver their own pages quickly, they are unlikely to be able to offer you a better service.

### What extra services do you offer?

Depending on the content of your Web site, you may require some extra services. For example, if you intend to use your site to sell things, you will need a hosting company that can make it safe for you to use your site to collect private information such as credit card details and telephone numbers.

You may expect a lot of the people that will use your site to access the Net through a type of digital telephone line known as Integrated Services Digital Network (ISDN) lines. If so, you should choose a company that has an ISDN connection to the Internet.

Make sure a hosting company can provide all the extra services you may require.

## What costs can I expect?

Make sure you understand exactly how much a company will charge to host your site. Most companies charge a monthly fee and some charge an initial set up fee too.

Hosting companies often offer a variety of deals, each with a different monthly fee. The price you pay will depend on the size of your site, the type of cables the hosting company uses, and any extra services you require.

## Are there any extra costs?

Sometimes a monthly fee doesn't include all the services you might require. For instance, a company may charge you extra each time you update your site. Try to find one that will let you change your site as often as you like for no extra cost.

Each time someone visits your site, a certain amount of computer data is copied from the server where your site is stored to their computer. Most of the prices quoted by hosting companies cover a limited amount of data transfer. If a lot of people visit your site or if it contains a lot of very large files, you may exceed this amount. Hosting companies usually record how much data is copied from your site each month and may charge you extra for going over the limit.

## Do you provide technical support?

You may need advice on how to transfer your site to the Web and how to maintain it. Find out if a company provides support for its clients and whether this is done by telephone or by e-mail. Make sure support will be available at the times when you are most likely to need it.

## Bandwidth

When two or more computers are connected, a channel for exchanging information is formed. The computers on the Net are connected by telephone networks, by fiber optic cables and by satellite. Different types of channels can transfer different amounts of data per second. The maximum amount of data a channel can transfer is known as its bandwidth capability.

*Communications satellite*

Hosting companies connect their servers to the Net in different ways. In general, hosting companies that use faster channels are more expensive.

*Fiber optic cables*

Most hosting companies use fiber optic cables to connect their servers to the Internet. These cables contain thin glass strands called optical fibers that carry data. There are four types of fiber optic cables and each type has a different bandwidth. T1 cables can transfer up to 1.5 megabytes of data per second (mbps), T2 can transfer up to 10 mbps, T3 can transfer up to 30 mbps and ATM can transfer up to 100 mbps.

Some hosting companies connect their servers to the Internet by ISDN. ISDN lines have a bandwidth of 128 kilobytes per second (kbps). Web users can only benefit from the speed of ISDN transfer if they use an ISDN line to connect to the Net and a computer with ISDN hardware and software.

*This is an ISDN terminal adaptor. It is a device that allows a computer to send and receive data across ISDN lines.*

# *Uploading your site*

This section shows you how to transfer your Web site files onto your hosting company's server. Copying files from your computer onto another computer on the Internet is called uploading. Files are usually uploaded using a method called File Transfer Protocol (FTP).

## FTP clients

To transfer files by FTP, you need a program called an FTP client. On page 97, there is a list of FTP clients that are available on the Internet.

When you open an FTP client, you will see a window divided into two parts, similar to the one shown below. The left part displays a list of the files that are stored on your computer, called the local computer. The right part is used to display the files that are stored on other computers, known as remote computers.

The first time you open your FTP client, the right part of the window will be blank. This is because your computer is not yet connected to a remote computer.

## Preparations

In order to upload your site, you have to connect your computer to your hosting company's computer. To instruct your FTP client to do this, you need to enter some information, such as the computer's address, into a dialog box. With WS_FTP, this dialog box appears each time you start the program. Your hosting company will tell you exactly what information you need to enter in order to connect to their computer.

## Connecting

Once you have given your FTP client this information, you are ready to connect your computer to the hosting company's server. Connect to the Internet in the usual way. Then click on the *Connect* button in your FTP client. When your FTP client has connected to the server, the files that are stored on the server will appear on the right side of the window.

*A window from an FTP client called WS_FTP*

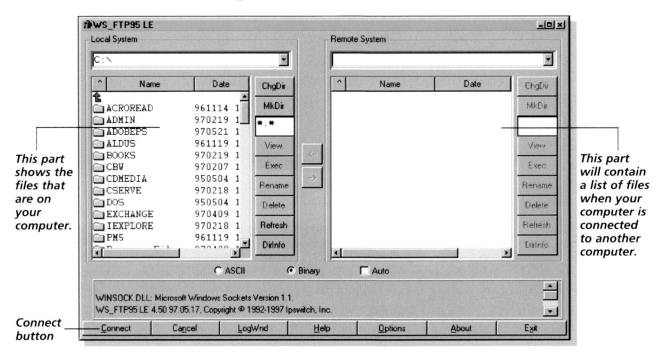

**This part shows the files that are on your computer.**

**Connect button**

**This part will contain a list of files when your computer is connected to another computer.**

## Transferring files

First use the left part of your FTP client's window to locate your Web site files on your computer's hard disk. You can open a directory or folder by double-clicking on its icon. Next use the right part of the window to open the directory on the server where you are going to store your Web site. Your

*Transferring files with WS_FTP*

*Use this button to upload files.*

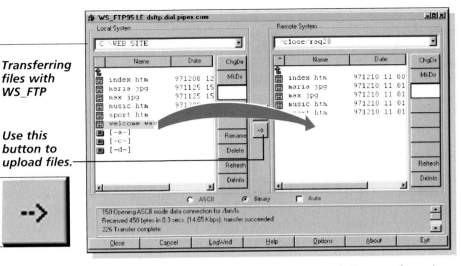

hosting company will tell you which directory you should use.

To transfer a file, select its filename with your mouse and click on the button which points to the right. You can select several files at once, but is is safest to transfer files one by one.

When a file has been successfully transferred to the server, its filename will appear in the right part of the window.

As soon as you have finished transferring a file, anyone with access to the Web can look at it as a Web page.

---

## After uploading

### Checking hyperlinks
Make sure that all the hyperlinks on your site work properly. To do this, connect to the Internet and download your home page by typing its URL into your browser's *Address* or *Location* box. Your hosting company will tell your what your home page's URL is. Once you have called up your home page, click on each of your site's links to check that it leads to the right page.

### Updating your site
To update your Web site, you have to change the source documents that are stored on your computer. When you are happy with the changes, transfer the new version of the files to the server. Your FTP client will automatically use these to replace the old versions.

### Publicizing your site
To enable other Web users to find your site, you should tell a selection of search engines about it (see page 96).

To do this, go to a search engine's home page and look for a hyperlink called Add URL or something similar. Click on this link to download a registration form. A search engine will use the information you enter onto its form to find and classify your site.

To avoid repeating this process many times, you can use a service that automatically submits the details of your site to several search services.

Hundreds of sites are added to the Web every day. A search engine won't be able to visit your site immediately. You may have to wait several weeks after registration for your site to appear in a search engine's index.

# Cyberchat

E-mail and newsgroups are great ways of using the Net to make friends and communicate, but you do have to wait for a reply. Sometimes it's only a couple of minutes, but it can be a day or two. Today, there are facilities on the Net that allow you to communicate with other users instantly.

## Internet phone

There are programs available that allow you to use your computer like a telephone. The Net can transmit sound in the same way that it transmits any other kind of data.

To talk to a friend on the Net, you will need a microphone, a pair of speakers connected to your computer, and a sound card (see page 11). The person you intend to talk to must have the same equipment. You will both need to download an Internet telephone program and you will have to pay for it.

Once you have installed your equipment and your program, you can dial up your friend's computer. When he or she answers, you can speak, just as on a normal telephone.

*This is an Internet phone called WebPhone.*

*You can dial a telephone number by clicking on these buttons on screen.*

One of the great advantages of using an Internet telephone is that you can call anywhere in the world for the price of the local call that connects your computer to your service provider's computer.

## Video phones

Internet video phones allow you not only to talk to a person via their computer, but also to see them on your computer screen while you talk.

To use this system you will need a video digitizer and a video camera connected to your computer system. This will film you and transmit the data over the Net to another user. You will also need a microphone, speakers, sound and video cards, and a video phone program.

## Conferencing

The Internet telephone and video phone systems described above have been further developed to allow several people to speak and watch each other at once. This enables people to have debates and discussions using the Net.

The quality of the sound and pictures achieved by these programs is getting better as the equipment and the speed of data transfer (see page 11) on the Net improves.

*CU-SeeMe is a program used for video-conferencing.*

### ✉ Finding software

You can find out where to go on the Net to download the software mentioned in this section in the list of sites and resources on page 97.

## Internet Relay Chat

A popular Net facility is Internet Relay Chat (IRC). This allows you to have live conversations with other users, using your keyboard to type your conversations. As you type a message, it instantly appears on another user's screen. He or she can read it and type a reply.

The groups in which people meet to have chats are called channels. Some of them are dedicated to discussions about particular topics, such as football or computer games, while others are used for more general, sociable chat.

The IRC channels are controlled by special computers on the Net called IRC servers, which transmit all the chatting around the world.

## IRC programs

To join in IRC, you will need a program called an IRC client program. This will interpret the data supplied by an IRC server. You can download an IRC client from the Net.

IRC is quite complicated to use. There are many codes and commands that you need to type in to tell your computer what you want it to do. So make sure that you read all the instructions that are downloaded with your IRC client program.

## Games on-line

If you like to play games on your computer, there are lots of challenging ones on the Net for you to download and play. But the best way of playing games is on-line, because you can play against other Net users. For example, a user in Berlin can play on-line chess against a user in Tokyo. If you prefer fantasy games, take part in adventures, fighting other users for prizes or teaming up with them to quest and battle together.

**Watch a game of on-line chess.**
**You could even take part yourself.**

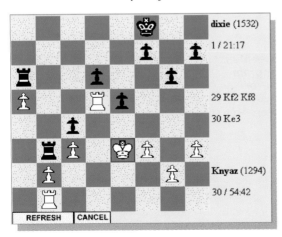

Multi-User Dungeons, known as MUDs, are popular on-line games, which take place in imaginary kingdoms. Most of them are text-based, but some have pictures.

To play an on-line game you need a piece of software called a client. This is a program which enables your computer to communicate with the computer on the Net on which a particular game program is running. You can find and download games clients like any other software from the Net. Most games pages on the Web have hyperlinks to sites where you can download client software.

The Net is also a good place to get in touch with other games enthusiasts so you can discuss tactics and expertise. There are many newsgroups and mailing lists dedicated to discussing individual games. The best place to start looking for a games newsgroup is in the rec.games folder in the list of newsgroups (see page 22).

# Virtual Reality on the Net

Virtual Reality (VR) is the use of computers to create objects and places which appear to be real. You can find some examples of Virtual Reality on Web pages.

## Virtual worlds

Anything which is created by Virtual Reality is known as a virtual world. A virtual world may be a planet, a group of buildings, or even a single room. It can be a copy of something which exists in the real world, or it can be something which is entirely imaginary. A virtual world is created with 3-D images.

On page 96, you will find the URLs of Web pages which contain hyperlinks to virtual worlds. It usually takes a few minutes to download one.

*A virtual world appears on your computer screen as a 3-D picture.*

*This virtual world is a copy of Piccadilly Circus, London.*

*This one is an imaginary space station.*

## Inside a virtual world

Use your mouse, or the arrow keys on your keyboard, to travel through a virtual world. You can explore the space in front and behind, on either side, or above and below you.

Wherever you go in a virtual world, it feels as though you are moving. This is because your surroundings change, just as they would in the real world. For example, when you approach an object, it appears to become bigger.

To make you feel as though you are moving closer, your computer draws a sequence of images. In each new image, the objects in front of you are slightly larger than in the previous one.

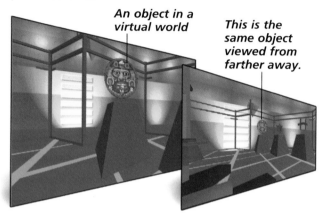

*An object in a virtual world*

*This is the same object viewed from farther away.*

Your computer has to draw each new image very quickly so you feel as if you are moving. If you have to wait for a new image to appear, the effect is lost. As a result, the images are usually quite simple.

As you explore a virtual world, you don't see yourself on your computer screen, you see only your surroundings.

## Hardware and software

To experience virtual worlds, you need a powerful computer (at least a 486DX66 with 16MB of RAM), a fast modem (at least 28.8 bps) and a video card.

You also need a browser that can handle a programming language called Virtual Reality Modeling Language (VRML). One such browser is Netscape Navigator 3.0. VRML is the language that is used to create most virtual worlds on the Web. If you don't have a VRML browser, you will need to obtain a VRML plug-in for your browser (see page 46).

*To visit a virtual world called AlphaWorld, you need a computer with a Pentium processor.*

## Meeting places

One of the most exciting things about virtual worlds on the Web is that you can use them to meet other people. A virtual world where you can see and communicate with other Web users is known as a 3-D chat room.

To enjoy 3-D chat rooms, you will have to download some software. You can find out more about this at:
**http://www.activeworlds.com/** or
**http://www.onlive.com/utopia/**.

*This 3-D chat room is based on Yellowstone National Park in the USA.*

## Avatars

Before you enter a 3-D chat room, you have to choose an "avatar". This is a character which will represent you in the virtual world. It may look like a person or an animal or an imaginary creature, such as an alien.

*Avatars from a virtual world called Utopia*

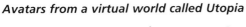

You use your arrow keys or your mouse to instruct your avatar to move. As you explore a 3-D chat room, you will see avatars which represent the other people who are visiting that particular virtual world at the same time as you.

## Communication

In some chat rooms, you use your keyboard to type what you want to say to the people you meet. Your words appear on the screen for them to read. In others, you can actually hear what other people are saying and talk to them.

*Avatars chatting in AlphaWorld*

## CD-ROMs

You can also buy virtual worlds on CD-ROM, which you can explore on- or off-line. The CD-ROM contains links to a Web server. If you go on-line to explore a world, you may meet other people there. You can only meet other people when you are on-line because the data which tells your computer what they are doing and saying is sent over the Net.

### ⚠ VRML problems

There are many different VRML browsers and plug-ins. Some virtual worlds only work with particular browsers and plug-ins. The only way to find out if your software can handle a virtual world is to visit it and see what happens.

If you can't see anything or if you can't move around, this means you don't have the right software for that particular world. You will have to download a different browser or plug-in and try again. Alternatively, look for a world which works with the software you already have.

# Future developments

Companies that develop software keep inventing and introducing exciting new ways of presenting information on the Internet.

Many of the things that you will be able to do with the Net in the future are already possible with very advanced computers. The technology will become available to most users once computers in homes, schools and offices become more powerful, and data can be transferred more quickly.

## Net links

The computers that make up the Net are linked in various ways: by telephone wires, by cables, and by satellites. Each type of link can transfer a maximum amount of data per second. This maximum limit is called bandwidth. It is measured in bps (see page 11).

Cable and satellite links are "high-speed" Internet connections. This means they have a large bandwidth. Most Net users still have data delivered to their computers by ordinary telephone wires. Some people, however, use high-speed connections.

## High-speed connections

The cables which are used to transfer data across the Internet are made of thin glass strands. They use pulses of light to transmit information. To use cables to send and receive Net data, you need a cable modem.

*Pulses of light passing along thin glass strands*

*A cable modem*

Information can be sent along these cables thousands of times faster than along ordinary copper telephone wires.

Satellite links have an even larger bandwidth than cables. Internet data is transferred by communications satellites. These are spacecraft which circle Earth, automatically sending and receiving information.

*A communications satellite*

## Improving links

To increase the speed of data transfer over the Net, telephone lines are gradually being replaced by cable and satellite links. This is a very long and expensive process, but it will make the Internet more efficient.

## Web TV

You will soon be able to watch TV on Web pages. One of the great things about Web TV is that it will be interactive, which ordinary TV isn't. When you watch a news bulletin on ordinary TV, the information that you hear and see has been chosen by a reporter. You can't ask for more information about the things that interest you, or ask questions about the things you don't understand.

With Web pages, you can make choices about what information you require by clicking on hyperlinks. Similarly, with Web TV, you will be able to choose what you watch by clicking on hyperlinks. For example, if you are watching a program about a planet called Saturn, and you don't know where it is, you will be able to click on a hyperlink to find out.

*You will be able to find out more about Saturn using hyperlinks on Web TV.*

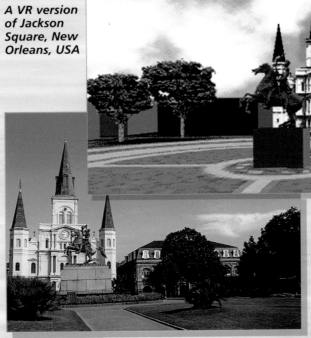

*A VR version of Jackson Square, New Orleans, USA*

## Virtual worlds

Some Net surfers are disappointed when they visit virtual worlds on the Web (see pages 84 and 85). They expect to find places in which there is a great deal to be discovered. In most virtual worlds, however, there are not many places to explore, and the pictures that make up the surroundings are not very detailed. However, as the speed at which data is transferred over the Internet increases, the quality of virtual worlds on the Web will improve.

*A photograph of the square*

*Compare the Virtual Reality Jackson Square to the real one. The 3-D image is not as detailed as the photograph.*

## Storage devices

On page 85 you found out that a virtual world can be stored on CD-ROM. Soon, virtual worlds will also be available on Digital Video Discs (DVD-ROM).

A DVD-ROM is a device on which a huge amount of information can be stored. A DVD-ROM looks like a CD-ROM, but it can hold up to 26 times more data.

Virtual worlds stored on DVD-ROM will be more detailed than the worlds that are currently available. Some DVD-ROM virtual worlds will contain links to Web servers. If you explore one of these worlds when you are on-line, you will be able to meet other Web users in highly realistic Virtual Reality environments. You will also be able to vary your environment by temporarily adding new objects. For example, if your virtual world was a forest, you could introduce birds that fly overhead.

*Digital video discs*

*This is a DVD-ROM drive, which is a device which reads DVD-ROMs. It fits into a computer's processing unit.*

# Problems and solutions

The Internet is sometimes called the Information Superhighway. This description gives many people high expectations of the speed at which information can travel via the Net. Some users are disappointed by problems and congestion which can make the Net slow and frustrating to use. They might call it the Information Dirt-track or the Information Superhypeway.

This section explores some of the problems you may come across on the Net and suggests how to deal with them.

## No connection

When you dial up your access provider to go on-line, you may fail to make a connection. The most common cause of this is that too many people are using your IAP's computer and so there are no lines left available. This often happens at times of the day when a lot of people want to use the Net. Redial a few times, but if this doesn't work, try again an hour later.

If you still can't get a connection, telephone your access provider to check that there isn't a fault with their computer.

If you often find that your access provider doesn't have enough telephone lines to deal with all their customers, you might consider finding an access provider with better facilities.

## Losing a connection

Once you are on-line, a message may appear telling you that you have lost your connection. This is usually due to your access provider's computer failing. Try connecting again.

## Problems on the Net

There are a number of reasons why you may be unable to download Web pages or files successfully. Here are some of them.

**Equipment failure**   The computers and equipment that make up the Net sometimes break down. All you can do is try again later.

**Wrong address**   A message, such as Host Not Found, may appear on your screen. This usually means that you have typed in the URL incorrectly. Check carefully that you have used the correct upper and lower case letters and punctuation.

**Change of address**   You may see a message telling you that the file you require doesn't exist. It may have been removed from the Net, relocated, or had its name changed. Try removing the part of the URL that specifies the exact filename. For example, you might want to look at a photograph with the following address: **http://www.imaginary.co.uk/users/ phil_jones/pix/png32.html**. If you typed this in and the file didn't appear, you should try removing the filename, **png32.html**. This might take you to a list of the photographs available and you could resume your search.

**No access**   When trying to use an FTP site, you may be denied access. This is because the computers which store FTP files limit the number of people who are allowed to use them at the same time. This ensures that downloading files doesn't get too slow. Try again later.

**Software problems**   If you can't get your browser to connect to anything, close it down and reopen it. There may be a mistake in the program, called a bug. This is particularly possible if you are using a beta version of a program (see page 45). If the problem persists, report it to the program's manufacturer.

## Congestion

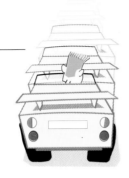

One of the main problems facing the Net is its growing popularity. Every day, more people want to go on-line and do increasingly complicated things, such as downloading video and sound clips. The result is that the Net gets congested with traffic jams of data. This makes every-thing move more slowly, just like cars on a busy road.

To cope with this problem, new high-speed connections are being built which can handle more data at greater speeds. But these improvements take time and money.

In the meantime, it's a good idea to avoid the busiest times on the Net, which tend to be when people in the USA are using it. This is because most of the resources on the Net are based in the USA.

### 🌐 How many?

People have calculated that if the number of Net users continues growing at its current rate, everyone in the world will be on-line by the year 2001. This is nonsense, of course, because in many countries people can't afford to buy computers.

## Cutting costs

Going on-line doesn't have to be expensive. You don't need to buy a high-speed modem, a super-fast computer or expensive software. Here are some ways in which you can enjoy all the Net has to offer without spending a fortune.

• If your computer isn't powerful, which means that it can't process data quickly, don't use a Web browser, like Netscape Navigator, that can access newsgroups and send e-mail as well as browse the Web. Programs like this are complicated, and will make your computer run slowly. Choose individual programs to use newsgroups, e-mails and FTP. These programs are older and simpler, and will use less of your computer's memory.

• If you don't have a high speed modem, make sure that you minimize the amount of data you need to download.

One way of doing this is to instruct your browser to download only the text of Web pages, not the pictures. This is because pictures can take a long time to download. You can find out how to do this on page 33.

• Remember that all the programs you will need to use the Internet are available free on the Net. You can find out the URL addresses of where to go to download some useful programs on page 97.

• If you are charged for the amount of time you that you spend connected to the Net, always write your e-mails and any messages that you want to send to newsgroups before you are connected up to the Net.

• If you are charged more for telephone calls made at certain times of the day it is a good idea to avoid using the Net at these times.

# Safety Net

With millions of people using the Net, there are bound to be those who misuse it. Here are some useful guidelines that will ensure the Net is a safe place for you to surf.

 Don't give your e-mail address to strangers. You don't want to receive lots of unwanted e-mail. Just think, you wouldn't give your snail mail address to a complete stranger, would you?

 Someone you chat to on the Net may suggest meeting up in real life (known as "boinking"). If you want to go, make sure you arrange to meet in a public place, where you will feel safe.

 You should always be aware that it is easy for people to play pranks or pretend to be something they aren't on the Net. For instance, you might meet an adult pretending to be a child.

 When you send information via the Net, it passes from one computer to another until it reaches its destination. If somebody gained access to a Net computer, they could use your information dishonestly. Don't send personal details, such as your home address, phone number, or financial details, such as a credit card number, via the Net.

There are some Web sites where financial details are safe. The information is coded so that it can't be used by anyone else.

 People are free to publish whatever they like on the Net. So, as well as interesting things, there's also unpleasant, unsuitable and dangerous information out there. Be careful to avoid anything you don't want to look at.

There are programs available that will check the information you download from the Net for offensive words, and block access to certain Web sites.

Computer viruses are programs which can damage the data stored on your computer. Every day new viruses are being invented by people who want to harm the Net.

Your computer can catch a virus over the Net if you copy files from an infected computer. Make sure that you have anti-virus software installed on your computer. This will check your hard disk for certain viruses. Update this software regularly to catch new viruses.

Hackers are people who access computer systems without permission. They can link up their own computers to networks, and open private files. By changing the information in these files, they may be able to steal money or goods.

If you have private information stored on your computer, make sure you set up your system to prevent people connecting to it. If you are using a computer at home, it is unlikely that people can access your files.

## Net potatoes

Some people predict that by the year 2000, people will spend more time surfing the Internet than they currently spend watching television.

Some Net facilities, such as games and IRC, can become very addictive. Remember, using a computer for any purpose for long periods of time can damage your health.

It's essential to take a ten minute break every hour that you use a computer. This will rest your eyes and other parts of your body.

There's more to life than surfing the Net. So make sure you don't become a Net potato and end up at the receiving end of a common Net insult... GAL, which means Get A Life!

# A glossary of Internet words

Here's a list of some of the Internet words you may come across and their meanings. The definitions are specific to the use of the words in relation to the Net. Some words have other meanings in different contexts.

Any word that appears in *italic* type is defined elsewhere in the glossary.

**acronym**   Words that are usually made up of the first letters of a phrase or saying, such as BFN, which is an acronym for Bye For Now.

**address**   A description of where to find a piece of information on the *Net*.

**AIFF**   A sound *file format* developed by a company called Apple Computers.

**alternative text**   Text that a *browser* displays instead of a picture.

**anchor tag**   An *HTML* instruction used to create *hyperlinks*.

**animation**   A moving image made by playing a series of pictures in quick succession.

**anonymous FTP**   To transfer files across the *Net* you need to use *FTP*. Anonymous FTP is when you can transfer them without using a special user code or password.

**applet**   A small program written in a programming language called *Java*. The applet might be inserted into a *Web page*.

**application**   A program that allows you to do something useful with your computer.

**archive**   A file or files that have been grouped together. They may have been compressed so that they are smaller.

**attachment**   A file, such as a picture file, sent with an *e-mail* message.

**AU**   A sound *file format*.

**audio player**   A program that plays sounds.

**avatar**   A small on-screen, movable picture which represents the body of a computer user in a *virtual world*.

**backup**   A copy of a computer program or a computer document.

**backbone**   A link between computers that carries a lot of information very quickly and usually over a long distance.

**bandwidth**   A measurement of the amount of data that can flow through a link between computers. It is usually measured in *bits* per second (*bps*).

**bar**   A long, thin picture used to divide up information on a *Web page*.

**betaware**   Newly written programs that are made available to be tested by users.

**bit**   The smallest unit of computer data.

**blockquote tag**   An *HTML* instruction used to distinguish quotations from the main text on a *Web page*.

**block level element**   A *tag* that is automatically followed by a paragraph break.

**body**   1. The part of an *e-mail* in which the message appears. 2. The part of a *Web page* which appears inside the main part of a *browser* window.

**boinking**   Meeting face-to-face someone with whom you have made contact on the *Net*.

**bounce**   When *e-mail* fails to get through to its destination.

**bps**   (bits per second). The unit used to measure how fast information is transmitted by a *modem*.

**browser**   A piece of software used to find and display documents stored on the *Internet*.

**bug**   An imperfection in a computer program.

**byte**   A unit of eight bits.

**cache**   The part of a computer's memory where *Web pages* that have been *downloaded* are stored temporarily.

**case-sensitive**   A word used to describe a program that is able to distinguish between capital and small letters.

**CGI script**   (Common Gateway Interface script). A type of program that processes information entered into a *form*. It may automatically create *Web pages* in response to this information.

**clickstream**   The path you take around the *Web* by clicking on *hyperlinks*.

**client**   A program that enables a computer to use the services provided by other computers.

**clip art**   Pictures that are publicly available for illustrating computer documents.

**compression**   Converting a file to a *format* that minimizes the amount of space it takes up on a disk.

**computer graphics**   Pictures created with a computer.

**counter**   A device that counts how many times a *Web page* is *downloaded* by *Net* users.

**country code**   The part of the name for a *Net* computer that indicates what country it is in.

**crash**   A sudden failure in a computer system.

**Cybercafés**   Cafés at which people can use computers to access the Net.

**cyberspace**   The imaginary space that you travel around in when you use the *Net*.

**decaffeinated**   Not containing *Java applets*.

**decompressor**   A program used to expand compressed files.

**dialer**   A program that instructs a *modem* to telephone another computer.

**dial up**   Use telephone lines to connect a computer to another computer on the *Internet*.

**digital**   A word used to describe information that is recorded as a number code that can be understood and processed by computers. It is also used to describe a device, such as a computer, that can process this number code.

**digitize**   The process of converting information into number code that can be processed by computers.

**DNS**   (Domain Name System). A system of giving computers on the *Net* names that are unique and easy for users to remember.

**domain**   Part of the name for an *Internet* computer that specifies its location and what sort of organization owns it.

**dots per inch**   A measure of *resolution*.

**down**   The word used to describe computer equipment that is not functioning.

**download**   To copy a file from a computer on the *Net* to your own computer.

**drilling down**   Going though the levels of a directory, choosing narrower and narrower subject areas.

**e-mail**   (electronic mail). A way of sending messages from one computer to another across a network.

**embed**   To place an object such as a picture or sound in a computer document.

**emoticon** *see* **smiley**

**encryption**   Using a complex code to keep information secret.

**expansion card**   A device, such as a *sound card*, that extends a computer's capabilities by enabling it to perform a particular task.

**FAQ**   (Frequently Asked Questions). A document used by *newsgroups, mailing lists* and *Web sites* which lists the answers to the questions commonly asked by new members.

**file format**   The way a program stores information on a disk.

**flame mail**   Angry or rude messages sent to a member or members of a *newsgroup*.

**follow up**   A message sent to a *newsgroup* commenting on a previously posted message.

**form**   A *Web page* on which you can enter information.

**frame**   One of a series of images that makes up an *animation*.

**freeware**   *Software* that is free to use.

**FTP**   (File Transfer Protocol). The system used to transfer files from one computer to another over the *Net*.

**FTP client**   A program that enables you to contact another computer on the *Internet* and exchange files with it.

**GIF**   (Graphical Interchange Format). A picture *file format* usually used for *computer graphics*.

**Gopher**   A program which searches the *Net* for information by picking options from menus.

**guestbook**   A device that allows visitors to a *Web site* to leave comments.

**GUI**   (Graphical User Interface). A system that uses on-screen pictures which can be clicked on with a mouse to give a computer instructions.

**hacker**   Someone who gains unauthorized access to a computer to look at, change or destroy data.

**handshake**   A signal set by a *modem* to an *access provider*'s computer in order to obtain permission to connect to the *Net*.

**hardware**   The equipment that makes up a computer or a *network*.

**header**   Information at the start of a document that tells a computer what to do with it.

**helper application**   A program which is automatically launched when a *browser* needs help performing a particular task. Helper applications are used for files which are too big or complicated for *plug-ins* to handle.

**hit**   A page found by a *search engine* which contains the *key words* entered into its *query box*. It can also mean when someone looks at a *Web site*. The number of hits a site receives can be counted to see how popular the site is.

**home page**   A page designed as a point of entry into a *Web site*.

**host**   A computer connected to the *Net* which holds information that can be accessed by users.

**HTML**   (HyperText Mark-up Language). The computer code added to word-processed documents to turn them into *Web pages*.

**HTTP**   (HyperText Transfer Protocol). The language computers use to transfer *Web pages* over the *Net*.

**hyperlink**   A piece of text, picture or graphic which links one *Web page* to another page.

**hypertext**   A word or group of words which are *hyperlinks*.

**icon**   A picture which you can click on to make your computer do something, or which appears to indicate that your computer is doing something.

**imaging software**   Software that allows you to create and edit *digital* images.

**Infobahn, Information Superhighway** Slang words for the *Internet*.

**in-line image**   A picture that appears on a *Web page*.

**intelligent agent**   (IA). A program which performs tasks on behalf of its user, and adapts itself to its user's preferences.

**Internet**   (or the Net). A computer *network* made up of millions of linked computers.

**Internet service providers** (ISPs) also known as **Internet access providers** (IAPs) Companies that sell *Net* connections to people.

**InterNIC**   An organisation that gives out and controls the use of *domain names*.

**invalid**   A word used to describe an out-of-date *hyperlink* or incorrect HTML.

**IP**   (Internet Protocol). The system used to specify how data is transferred over the *Net*.

**IP address**   The unique number given to each computer on the *Net*.

**IRC**   (Internet Relay Chat). A way of having a conversation with other *Net* users by typing messages and reading their responses.

**ISDN**   (Integrated Services Digital Network). A type of high speed telephone line which can transmit data between computers very quickly.

**Java**   A programming language which works on all computers. It is used to add animations and interactive features to *Web pages*.

**JPEG format**   A picture *file format* that is usually used for storing images.

**key word**   A word that is essential to a document's content.

**kilobyte**   Approximately 1,000 *bytes*.

**link**   1. A connection between two computers. 2. The highlighted text or pictures on a *Web page*.

**link checker**   A program that tests *hyperlinks* to find out whether they are still valid.

**local system**   The computer at which a user is working, as opposed to a *remote system*.

**location box** (also known as an **address box**)   The part of your *browser* where the *URLs* of *Web pages* are displayed.

**log on/log in**   Connect a computer to another computer.

**lurking**   Reading the messages sent to a *newsgroup* without sending any yourself.

**mailbox**   The place where *e-mail* is kept for a user by an *Internet service provider*.

**mailing list**   A discussion group where messages are posted to its members via *e-mail*.

**mail server**   A computer that handles *e-mail*.

**mbps**   *Megabytes* per second.

**megabyte**   Approximately 1 million *bytes*.

**mega tag**   A *tag* that helps a *search engine* classify a *Web page*.

**microphone**   A device that converts sound into electrical signals that can be processed by a computer.

**MIDI** (Musical Instrument Digital Interface). A method for the exchange of information between computers and electronic musical instruments.

**modem** (MOdulate/DEModulate). A device that allows computer data to be sent down a telephone line.

**Netiquette** Rules about the proper way to behave when using the *Net*.

**Net surfing or surfing on the Net**
Exploring the *Net* by jumping from one file to another, like a surfer catching one wave after another.

**network** A number of computers and other devices that are linked together so that they can share information and equipment.

**network computer** A special computer designed exclusively to be used on a *network* such as the *Net*.

**Network Information Center** (NIC). An organization that controls *domain names*.

**newbie** A new *Net* user or new member of a *newsgroup*.

**newsgroup** A place where people with the same interests can *post* messages and see other people's responses.

**newsreader** A program that lets you send and read the messages in *newsgroups*.

**node** Any computer attached to the *Net*.

**off-line** Not connected to the *Net*.

**on-line** Connected to the *Net*.

**on-line service** A company that gives you access to its private *network*, as well as access to the *Internet*.

**operator** A word or symbol which gives a particular instruction to a *search engine*.

**ordered list** A numbered list on a *Web page*.

**packet** A chunk of information sent over the *Net*.

**page** A document or chunk of information available on the *Web*.

**pixel** (picture element). A tiny dot that is part of a picture. Everything that appears on a computer screen is made up of pixels.

**platform** A combination of the type of hardware that a computer is made from, such as IBM PC compatible or Macintosh, and the type of operating system that controls it.

**plug-in** A program you can add to your *browser* that enables it to perform extra functions, such as displaying video clips.

**POP** (Point Of Presence). A point of access to the *Net*, usually a computer owned by an *Internet service provider*.

**post** Placing a message in a *newsgroup* so that other members can read it.

**protocol** A set of rules that two computers use when communicating with each other.

**public domain images** Pictures that do not belong to a particular person or organization. A user does not need permission to use them.

**query** Instructions, made up of *key words* and *operators*, that you give to a *search engine* so it can find *Web pages* on a particular subject.

**query box** The place on a *search engine*'s *home page* where you type your *query*.

**register** To type details about yourself on a *form* on a *Web site* in order to gain access to the information on that site.

**remote system** The computer to which a user is connected by a *modem* and a telephone line.

**resolution** The number of *pixels* that make up a picture on a computer's screen.

**scanner** A machine used to copy a picture or some text from paper onto a computer.

**search engine** A program within a *Web page* that locates other pages containing particular words or phrases.

**security** The protection of information so that unauthorised users can't look at it or copy it.

**serial port** The part of a computer through which data can be transmitted.

**server** A computer that carries out certain tasks for other computers on a *network*. Some servers store information that all the computers on the network use. Others link individual computers or small networks to big networks.

**set-top box** A piece of computer equipment that connects to your TV and lets you access the *Net* using the TV as a screen.

**shareware**   Software which you can try out before you have to pay for it.

**shouting**   Writing messages in UPPER CASE letters lets everyone know that you are angry.

**signature file**   A file, often a picture or a quotation, attached to the end of an *e-mail*.

**smiley**   A picture, made up from keyboard characters, used to add emotion to a message.

**snail mail**   Normal mail delivered by the post office, as opposed to *e-mail* sent over the *Net*.

**sound card**   A device that enables a computer to capture sound and play it back.

**source code**   The *HTML* code that makes up a particular *Web page*.

**spamming**   Sending lots of messages to a *newsgroup*, a *mailing list* or an individual.

**stale link**   A *hyperlink* to a document that has been deleted or moved.

**statistics log**   A record of information about the way a particular *Web site* is used. It is stored on the same computer as the *Web site*.

**subscribe**   Add your address to a *mailing list* or *newsgroup*.

**tag**   An *HMTL* instruction that tells a *browser* how to display a certain part of a document.

**TCP/IP**   The language which computers on the *Net* use to communicate with each other.

**Telnet**   A program that allows you to connect your computer to another computer so that you can interact with it.

**terminal adaptor**   A device that connects a computer or a fax machine to an *ISDN* system.

**text editor**   A program that can produce text documents.

**text level element**   A *tag* that affects the appearance of a piece of text on a *Web page*.

**thread**   A sequence of messages sent to a *newsgroup* forming a discussion on a subject.

**thumbnail**   A small version of a picture.

**tiling**   The repeated use of a small picture to fill a larger space.

**timeout**   When a computer gives up attempting to carry out a particular function, because it has taken too long.

**trialware**   Software which you can try out for free before having to pay for it.

**unordered list**   A list on a *Web page* that appears with bullet points.

**up**   A word used to describe a computer that is functioning.

**upload**   To copy files, via the *Internet,* from your computer onto another computer.

**URL**   (Uniform or Universal Resource Locator).  The system by which all the different resources on the *Net* are given an address.

**Usenet**   A collection of *newsgroups*.

**validator**   A program that tests *HTML* to see whether it is correct or not.

**video card** (also known as **graphics card**) A device that enables a computer to show text and pictures on its screen.

**Virtual Reality**   (VR). The use of 3-D computer pictures to draw places and objects that you can move around.

**virtual world**   A place created by a computer.

**virus**   A program specially designed to interfere with other programs and files.

**VRML**   (Virtual Reality Modeling Language). A programming language used to create *virtual worlds.*

**WAV**   A sound *file format* developed by a company called Microsoft.

**Web editor**   (also known as **HTML editor**) A program that helps to create *Web pages.*

**Web master**   A person who creates or maintains a *Web site*.

**Web page**   A computer document written in *HTML* and linked to other computer documents by *hyperlinks*.

**Web site**   A collection of *Web pages*, set up by an organisation or an individual, that are usually stored on the same computer.

**word processing program**   A program that can produce text documents with complex layouts and different styles of letters.

**World Wide Web** (also known as **WWW** or the **Web**)   A vast collection of information available on the *Net*. The information is divided up into *Web pages* which are joined by *hyperlinks.*

**zip**   A program used to compress files to make them smaller.

# Useful addresses

Here is a selection of Web sites which you might like to visit. Some of them contain more information about things which are mentioned in this book. Others are sites which are featured in the book or which are particularly interesting to visit.

## Internet access providers

The Directory, links to access proviers' sites worldwide:
**http://www.thedirectory.org/**

## Computing magazines

PC Magazine Online:
**http://www.zdnet.com/pcmag/**

ZDNet Mac:
**http://www.zdnet.com/mac/**

C/Net:
**http://www.cnet.com/**

## Further information

About intelligent agents:
**http://www.agentware.com/**
**http://firefly.com/**

About digital money:
**http://www.digicash.com**
**http://www.cybercash.com**

About safety issues:
**http://www.safekids.com/**

About Real Audio sites and live concerts on the Web:
**http://www.timecast.com/**

Web design tutorials for beginners:
**http://www.w3.org/MarkUp/**
**http://werbach.com/barebones/**

Addresses of virtual worlds:
**http://planet9.com/**
**http://hiwaay.net/~crispen/vrml/worlds.html**

## Search services

Altavista:
**http://www.altavista.digital.com/**
HotBot:
**http://www.hotbot.com/**
Lycos:
**http://www.lycos.com/**
OpenText:
**http://www.opentext.com/**
WebCrawler:
**http://www.webcrawler.com/**
Yahoo!:
**http://www.yahoo.com/**

Search engines for software:
**http://www.shareware.com/**
**http://www.download.com/**

Site that submit URLs to search services:
**http://www.submit-it.com/**
**http://www.powerpromote.com/**

## Entertainment

Disney's home page:
**http://www.disney.com/**

Nintendo's home page:
**http://www.nintendo.com/**

Kidlink, on-line chat for kids:
**http://www.kidlink.org/IRC/**

Lists of interesting sites for children:
**http://www.ability.org.uk/children.html**

## Software

Here is a selection of sites where you will find software to download from the Net:

### Operating systems
Windows 95:
**http://www.windows95.com/**
Macintosh:
**http://wwwhost.ots.utexas.edu/mac/internet.html**

## Software for compressing files
PKZip:
**http://pkware.com/**
Winzip for Windows:
**http://www.winzip.com/**
StuffIt for Macs:
**http://onyx.aladdinsys.com/expander/expander1.html**

## Communications software
WebPhone:
**http://www.netspeak.com/**
CU-SeeMe:
**http://cu-seeme.cornell.edu/**

## Web editors
Adobe PageMill: **http://www.adobe.com/**
Claris Home Page: **http://www.claris.com/**
DreamWeaver: **http://www.macromedia.com/**
For Windows only:
Hotdog Pro: **http://www.sausage.com/**
Microsoft Front Page: **http://www.microsoft.com/**
For Macintosh only:
BB Edit: **http://www.barebones.com/**

## Image editing software
For Windows only:
L View: **http://www.lview.com/**
JASC's Paintshop Pro: **http://www.jasc.com/**
For Macintosh only:
GraphicConverter: **http://www.goldinc.com/Lemke/**

## GIF animation editors
For Windows only:
WebImage:
**http://www.group42.com/webimage.htm**
Ulead GIF Animator:
**http://www.unlead.com/**
For Macintosh only:
GIF Builder:
**http://www.iawww.epfl.ch/Saff/Yves.Piguet/**
**clip2gif-home/GifBuilder.html**

## Sound editing programs
CoolEdit:
**http://www.syntrillium.com/**
Cubase:
**http://www.steinberg.net/**
Mixman Studio:
**http://www.mixman.com/**

## FTP Clients
For Windows only:
WS_FTP: **http://www.ipswitch.com/**
CuteFTP: **http://www.cuteftp.com/**
For Macintosh only:
Fetch: **http://www.dartmouth.edu/pages/softdev/**

## Other
Netscape Navigator®: **http://www.netscape.com/**
Microsoft®Internet Explorer: **http://www.microsoft.com/**

A program for creating Java applets:
**http://www.jamba.com/index.html**

InfoLink, a link checker:
**http://www.biggbyte.com/**

## Web Resources

Here is a list of sites from which you might like to add to your Web pages:

Pictures and animations:
**http://www.w3.org/Icons/**
**http://www.barrysclipart.com/**
**http://vr-mall.com/anigifpd/anigifpd.html**

Backgrounds:
**http://www.netscape.com/assist/net_sites/bg/backg**
**rounds.html**
**http://www.meat.com/textures/**

Java applets:
**http://www.javaboutique.internet.com/**

Sounds:
**http://www.sounddogs.com/**
**http://www.microsoft.com/gallery/files/sounds/**
**default.htm**

Color codes:
**http://www.imagitek.com/hex/**
**http://www.prgone.com/colors/**
**http://aloe.com/colors.htm**

Counters and guestbooks:
**http://www.freecount.com/**
**http://www.pagecount.com/**
**http://www.guestworld.com/**

# Acknowledgements

Every effort has been made to trace the copyright holders of the material in this book. If any rights have been omitted, the publishers offer their sincere apologies and will rectify this in any subsequent editions following notification.

Usborne Publishing Ltd. has taken every care to ensure that the instructions contained in this book are accurate and suitable for their intended purpose. However, they are not responsible for the content of, and do not sponsor, any Web site not owned by them, including those listed below, nor are they responsible for any exposure to offensive or inaccurate material which may appear on the Web.

Microsoft, Microsoft Windows, Microsoft Internet Explorer and Microsoft FrontPage are registered trademarks of Microsoft Corporation in the US and other countries. Screen shots and icons reprinted with permission from Microsoft Corporation.

Netscape, Netscape Navigator, and the Netscape N logo are registered trademarks of Netscape Communications Corporation in the US and other countries. Netscape Messenger and Netscape Composer are also trademarks of Netscape Communications Corporation, which may be registered in other countries.

Cover: Gateway P5-200 Multimedia PC. Photograph reproduced with permission from Gateway 2000.
p.6 and p.7 Rusti Sprokit. All rights copyright © 1996 crisp wreck. Unauthorized reproduction and/or sale is prohibited and subject to intergalactic criminal prosecution. Used by permission. WebPhone is a trademark of NetSpeak Corporation. Patents pending.
http://www.netspeak.com/
RadioNet. Copyright © 1996 T.P.I. GmbH - the mediaw@re company - designed by Klaus Eisermann.
http://www.radio-net.com/hpengl.htm
Visible Human Project.
http://www.nlm.nih.gov/research/visible/
The White House for Kids.
http://www1.whitehouse.gov/WH/kids/html/kidshome.html
The Art of China.
http://pasture.ecn.purdue.edu/~agenhtml/agenmc/china/china.html
CU-SeeMe. Copyright © 1993, 1994, 1995, Cornell University.
http://cu-seeme.cornell.edu/
AlphaWorld. Copyright © 1995-1996 Worlds Inc.
http://www.activeworlds.com/
The original unofficial Elvis home page.
http://sunsite.unc.edu/elvis/elvishom.html
Cyberkids. Copyright © 1995-96 Mountain Lake Software, Inc. Used with permission.
http://www.cyberkids.com/
Eurostar. Used with permission.
http://www.eurostar.com/eurostar/
World Bank. Copyright © The International Bank for Reconstruction and Development/The World Bank.
http://www.worldbank.org/
Europe Online map. Copyright © 1996 Europe Online S.A.
p.9 Computer Network connections on the NSFNET © NCSA, University of Illinois/Science Photo Library.
Cyberia Paris. Copyright © Frederick Froument.
p.10 Multimedia PC supplied by Gateway 2000 Europe.
p.11 Driving wheel supplied by Thrustmaster® Inc.
p.14 CompuServe.

http://www.compuserve.com/
Demon.
http://www.demon.net/
Pipex.
http://www.uunet.pipex.com/
Individual Network e.V.
http://www.north.de/ings/
America Online.
http://www.aol.com/
p.16 Pipex Dial screen shots Copyright © Pipex Dial is a registered trade mark of the Public Exchange Ltd trading as UUNET Pipex. All rights reserved.
p.28 and p.29 Biker Mice from Mars. Copyright ©1997 Brentwood Television Funnies, Inc.
© Columbia TriStar Interactive. All Rights Reserved. Visit the Sony Pictures Entertainment Web site at www.spe.sony.com.
Pie charts. Copyright (c) 1996 Creatonic Network.
http://www.creatonic.com
Super Mario. Used with permission of THE Games.
MTV. With thanks to MTV Online.
Mona Lisa. Copyright © Louvre, Paris/ET Archive.
BMW. Copyright ©1997 BMW (GB) Ltd.
Spinning globe. Copyright ©Tony Stone Images.
p.30 and 64 With thanks to Nasa.
http://www.nasa.gov/
p.32 The LEGO illustrations are used with the permission of the LEGO Group.
http://www.LEGO.com/
p.34 Cyber Tiger. Copyright ©1997 National Geographic Society. All rights reserved.
http://www.nationalgeographic.com/
Young Composers graphic reprinted with permission from Mountain Lake Software, Inc.
http://www.youngcomposers.com/
p.35 GARFIELD. Copyright © Paws, Inc. Dist by UNIVERSAL PRESS SYNDICATE. Reprinted with permission. All rights reserved.
p.36, 42, 56 and 68 YAHOO! and the YAHOO! logo are trademarks of YAHOO!, Inc. Text and artwork copyright ©1996 by YAHOO! Inc. All rights reserved.
http://www.yahoo.com/
p.37 With thanks to the National Museum of Natural History, Smithsonian Institution.
http://nmnhwww.si.edu/
Natural History Museum screen. Copyright © The Natural History Museum, London.
http://www.nhm.ac.uk/
p.38 TEENAGE MUTANT NINJA TURTLES™ is a trademark owned and licensed by Mirage Studios. Used with permission.
Turtle Trax photograph. Copyright © Ursula Keuper Bennett and Peter Bennett.
http://www.turtles.org/
Gulf of Maine Aquarium screen reproduced with permission of the Gulf of Maine Aquarium.
http://www.octopus.gma.org/
AltaVista. AltaVista and the AltaVista logo are trademarks or service marks of Compaq Computer Corporation. Used with permission.
http://www.altavista.digital.com/
p.39 Bon Jovi. Copyright © London Features International Ltd.
Spider. Nick Garbutt/Planet Earth Pictures.
P.40 Leaning Tower of Pisa. Life File/Emma Lee.
Fashion pictures. With thanks to Benetton.
http://www.benetton.com/

# Index

First published in 1998 by Usborne Publishing Ltd, Usborne House,
83-85 Saffron Hill London EC1N 8RT, England.
www.usborne.com

Copyright © 1997, 1998 Usborne Publishing Ltd. The name Usborne and
the device ⬤ are Trade Marks of Usborne Publishing Ltd.
All rights reserved. No part of this publication may be reproduced, stored in a
retrieval system or transmitted in any form or by any means, electronic,
mechanical, photocopying, recording or otherwise, without the prior permission
of the publisher. AE
First published in America in 1999
Printed in Spain